10

JUNIOR CLASSICS

Published by
Rupa Publications India Pvt. Ltd 2016
7/16, Ansari Road, Daryaganj
New Delhi 110002

Sales centres:
Bengaluru Chennai
Hyderabad Jaipur Kathmandu
Kolkata Mumbai Prayagraj

This is a work of fiction. Names, characters, places and incidents are either the product of the author's imagination or are used fictitiously and any resemblance to any actual person, living or dead, events or locales is entirely coincidental.

P-ISBN: 978-81-291-3894-1
E-ISBN: 978-81-291-4604-5

Third impression 2023

10 9 8 7 6 5 4 3

Printed in India

Contents

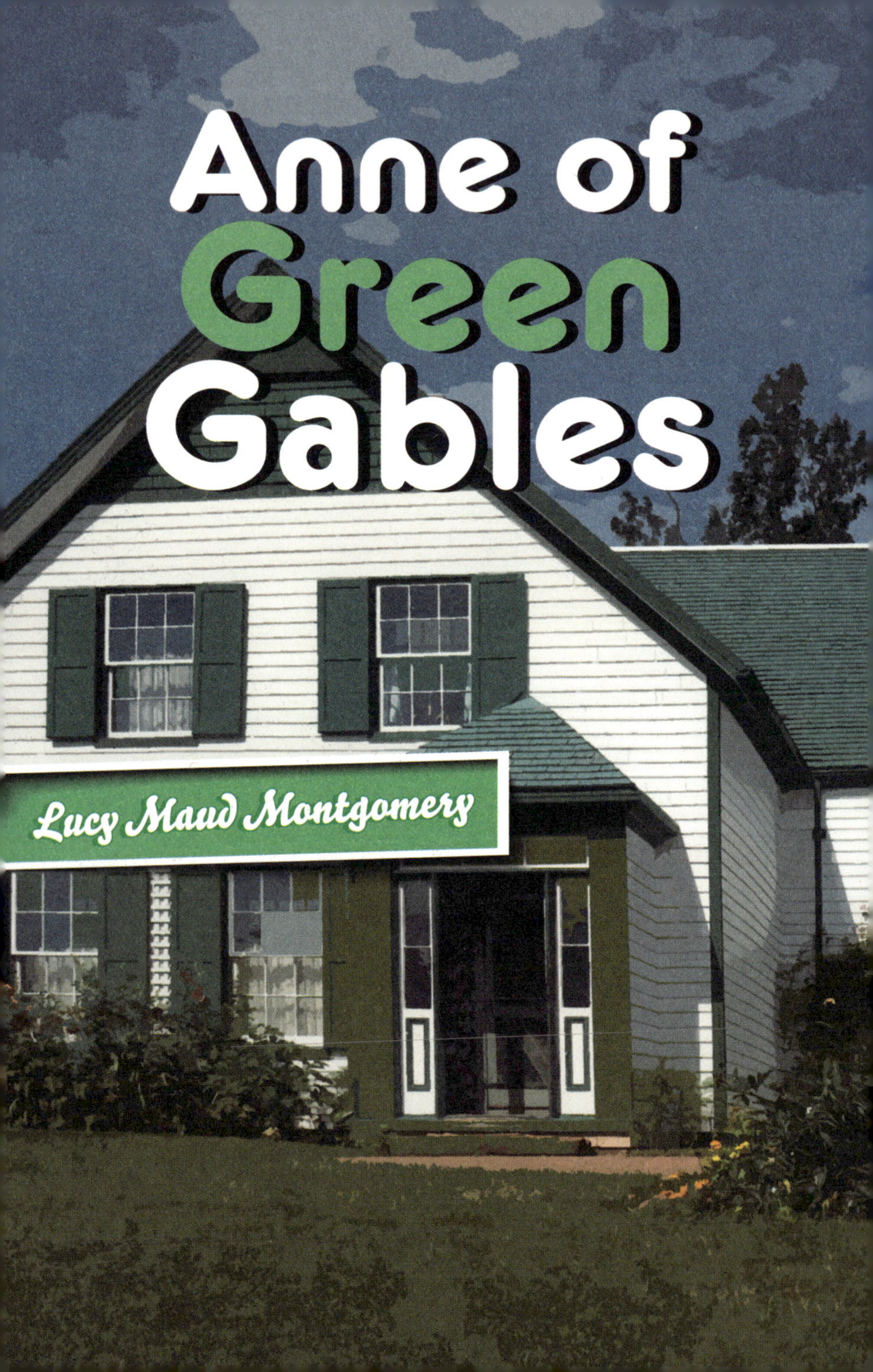
Anne of
Green
Gables
Lucy Maud Montgomery

In Avonlea, there were people who could look into their neighbours' business, and neglect their own. But the town's busybody Mrs Rachel Lynde was more capable than them, she had the remarkable ability to mind her own business and others' too, at the same time. Mrs Lynde was an outstanding housewife; she helped run the Sewing Circle and the Sunday school and was, besides, the strongest pillar of the Foreign Missions Auxiliary and Church Aid Society. But she still found plenty of time to sit by her window for hours, knitting cotton quilts, and keeping an eagle's eye on the main road.

One bright, sunny afternoon in June, Mrs Lynde was sitting by the window. Her husband Thomas Lynde, a timid little man, was sowing a turnip seed on the field beyond the barn. It was then she saw Matthew Cuthbert—who was also supposed to be doing the same as he had told Peter Morrison the day before in William J Blair's shop—was driving his carriage up the hill, which meant that he was going out of town. What's more, he was wearing his hat and the best set of clothes.

'Where and why was Matthew Cuthbert going?' Mrs Lynde asked herself.

'I'll go to Green Gables and ask Marilla where Matthew has gone,' Mrs Lynde, now completely excited, told herself.

So, after having her tea, Mrs Lynde took off to the Cuthberts' house. Green Gables was tucked away far from the public eye. Mrs Rachel Lynde used to say that living there was not living—'It's simply staying!' she said.

Marilla was Matthew's sister. She was tall and thin. She had dark hair with streaks of grey which she always tied up into a tight knot. She was a strict person but she had little experience of life. Neither of the siblings had ever married.

After exchanging pleasantries, Mrs Lynde said, 'I thought you were not well…when I saw Matthew rush off in his carriage.'

Marilla had been expecting Mrs Lynde.

She said, 'Matthew has gone to Bright River. We are getting a small boy for the farm work from an orphanage in Nova Scotia. He's arriving on the night train.'

Mrs Lynde was astonished. She remained speechless for a full five seconds.

Are you serious?' she asked.

'Of course,' said Marilla coolly, as if boys coming from orphanages were a normal part of spring work on any Avonlea farm.

***

Meanwhile, Matthew Cuthbert was enjoying the ride—except when he encountered a woman. He was very shy in front of any woman; in fact, with the exception of Mrs Lynde and Marilla, he dreaded women! He felt women were always laughing at him in secret. In this he may have been right for he was an odd man of sixty years, who had an awkward figure, long grey hair and a brown beard.

At the Bright River station, no train was in sight. The only creature on the long platform was a little girl who was seated on some gravel.

Matthew asked the stationmaster when the five-thirty train would arrive.

'The train arrived and left half an hour back,' was the answer he got. 'A passenger got off—for you. A small girl—she's sitting on the gravel.'

'I was expecting a boy,' said Matthew. 'Mrs Alexander Spencer was supposed to bring the boy from Nova Scotia for me.'

The stationmaster drew in his breath and whistled.

'Mrs Spencer came with that girl and put her in my charge. She told me that you and your sister intended to adopt her. That's all that I know about the matter.'

She watched Matthew intensely, a child of eleven who was dressed in a tight and ugly yellowish-grey dress. She had an old brown sailor hat on and two braids of thick red hair. Her small, thin and white face was full of freckles. Her eyes and mouth were large, the former green or grey, depending on the light and her moods.

Matthew was spared the trial of having to speak first for the girl held out her hand to him and said in a clear, sweet tone, 'You must be Mr Matthew Cuthbert of Green Gables. I'm very happy to see you. I thought you weren't coming, and I was imagining all kinds of horrible things that may have kept you.'

'I'm sorry I am late,' Matthew said shyly. 'Let me carry your bag.'

The child cheerfully replied, 'I'll carry it, it's not heavy. All my goods are in it, but it's not heavy. Also, if it is not carried in a particular way, the handle comes out.'

The girl kept on chatting too much about the bag being an old one, about the long drive to the Cuthbert's, how she loved driving, on and on she went.

She only stopped chatting because she was out of breath and they had reached the carriage.

Matthew was surprised that he was enjoying the little girl's company. Like most folks who hardly speak, he liked talkative folk, but had never thought that he would like the chattering of a small girl!

The girl enjoyed the scenic drive. She enjoyed every bit of the foliage that they passed by especially the 'Avenue'.

When they reached Green Gables, the yard was dark and the poplar leaves rustled silkily round it.

'The trees are talking in their sleep. Listen to them, they must be dreaming,' whispered the girl.

***

Marilla rushed forward when Matthew entered the house, but she was amazed to see the little red-haired girl in the ugly dress and eager, bright eyes.

'Who's that, Matthew?' she asked. 'And where's the boy?'

'Only she was there at the station, there was no boy,' said poor Matthew.

'But we told Mrs Spencer to bring along a boy!' said Marilla.

'Well, she brought her. I had to bring her home. She couldn't be left alone, no matter what mistake had been committed.'

As this dialogue went on, the child remained silent, her eyes shifting from Matthew to Marilla and she was visibly saddened. Suddenly she understood the meaning of what had been said.

'You don't want me for I'm not a boy! I should have expected that. Nobody ever wanted me. It was too good to last. I'm going to start crying!' she said.

Bursting into tears, she sank into a chair and buried her face on the table nearby.

Matthew and Marilla didn't know what to do or say. Finally Marilla spoke up, rather lamely, 'Well, you don't have to cry so much about it.'

The child lifted her head and exclaimed, 'This is the most tragical thing that has ever happened to me!'

Marilla smiled with hesitation.

'Stop crying. We won't turn you out tonight. We'll first investigate this matter. What's your name?'

'Will you call me Cordelia?' she asked eagerly.

'That's your name?'

'No-o-o, but it's really an elegant name.'

'If your name isn't Cordelia, what is it?'

'Anne Shirley,' the girl unwillingly said.

'We want a boy to assist Matthew on the farm. A girl is of no use to us.'

After Anne was sent to her bedroom, Marilla told her brother, 'You, or I, will have to meet Mrs Spencer tomorrow. Anne has to return to the orphanage.'

Matthew Cuthbert did not want Anne to leave. He told Marilla, 'I'll hire a French boy for the farm and Anne can give you company.' She's such a fascinating girl!'

But his sister firmly turned down that suggestion. That night the lonely, friendless and sad Anne cried herself to sleep.

The next day, she awoke to a beautiful morning and was enjoying the sights and smells when Marilla rudely told her to get dressed. Marilla did not really mean to be rude with the child but she just did not know how to talk with her. In the afternoon Matthew and Marilla set off with Anne.

***

Anne shared a secret, 'I've decided to enjoy this ride. I believe that you can almost always take pleasure from things if you firmly decide that you will.'

Marilla proceeded to learn everything she needed to know about Anne.

'No imaginings—just stick to bare facts,' she insisted.

So Anne told her, 'I was born in Bolingbroke, Nova Scotia, and turned eleven in March. My father, Walter Shirley, was a school teacher and my mother was named Bertha Shirley. They had such nice names!'

'My mother was also a teacher in the high school but she left her job after marrying. They were very poor, Mrs Thomas said. They lived in a small house in Bolingbroke. Mrs Thomas said I was tiny and skinny and all eyes, but mother felt I was beautiful.

'My mother died of fever three months after I was born and my father passed away four days after that, from fever too. I was left an orphan, and folks were wondering what to do with me. Finally, Mrs Thomas agreed to take me in, despite being poor and having a drunken husband. I was brought up by hand, that is, Mrs Thomas scolded me every time I did something wrong.

'The Thomases moved to Marysville and I stayed with them till I was eight. I helped to look after their children. They were four—all younger than me and it took a lot to look after them. Then Mr Thomas died in a train accident. His mother said she would take Mrs Thomas and the kids, but not me. Mrs Hammond said she would take me as she saw that I was useful with children. So I went to live with her in a small clearing. It was very lonely. Mr Hammond worked at a sawmill and Mrs Hammond had eight children—including three sets of twins! I lived with Mrs Hammond for more than two years. Then her husband died, and Mrs Hammond divided her kids among her relatives and migrated to the States. I went to the orphanage at Hopeton. They did not want me there; they said the place was overcrowded. They kept me for four months, however, and then Mrs Spencer came along.'

On hearing Anne's story, Marilla's heart melted. What an unloved, starved life this child had had—a life of poverty, too much work and neglect.

Marilla thought, 'No wonder she was so happy at the prospect of an actual home for herself.' Suppose she, Marilla, allowed Anne to stay with them?'

'She talks too much. But she can be trained,' she told herself.

***

When they reached Mrs Spencer's big yellow house they received a warm welcome.

'You're the last people I was expecting,' said Mrs Spencer.

Marilla said, 'There's been some mistake. Matthew and I told your brother Robert that we wanted a boy for our farm.'

Mrs Spencer said, 'I don't think you'll have to send the girl back. Mrs Peter Blewett said she badly wanted a little girl to work for her. Anne will be just right for her!'

Anne knew Mrs Peter Blewett as a complaining woman and had heard that she was 'a hard driver'.

Mrs Spencer suddenly exclaimed, 'If that isn't Mrs Peter herself coming up the path this very minute!'

But Marilla suffered pangs of guilt at having to give Anne to this woman, so she told Mrs Spencer that she would have to discuss the matter with Matthew and returned to Green Gables with Anne.

There she said to her brother, 'An old maid like me does not know much about bringing up children, but I can do better than an old bachelor!'

Matthew was delighted by Marilla's decision.

***

Marilla was shocked when Anne told her that night, 'I don't say prayers.'

'Do you know about God?' Marilla asked.

'God is an eternal and infinite spirit, unchangeable, in His wisdom, being, power, justice, holiness, truth and goodness,' the little girl replied.

A relieved Marilla said, 'Well, you're not an atheist. Where did you study religion?'

'At Sunday school at the orphanage.'

Marilla resolved to start Anne's religious teaching right away.

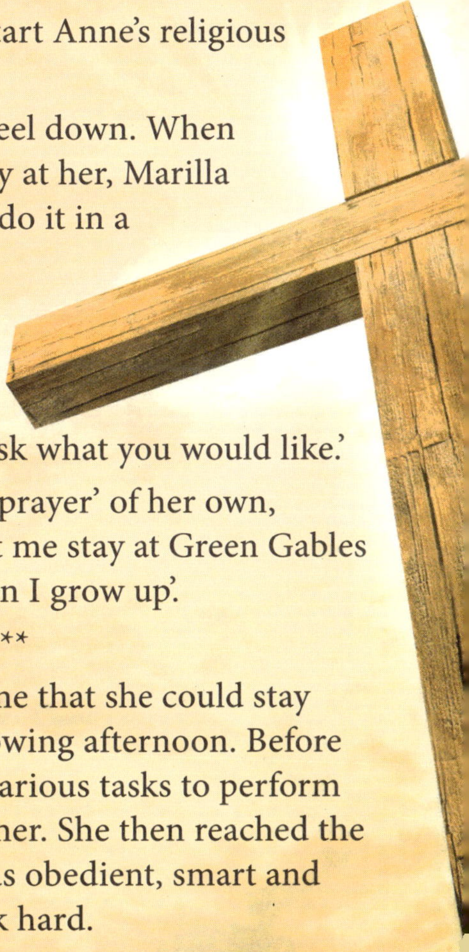

She made the girl kneel down. When Anne looked up seriously at her, Marilla knew she would have to do it in a unique way.

She finally said, 'Anne, pray your way. Thank God for what you've got and humbly ask what you would like.'

Anne then recited a 'prayer' of her own, asking God to 'please, let me stay at Green Gables and make me pretty when I grow up'.

***

Marilla only told Anne that she could stay at Green Gables the following afternoon. Before that, she gave the child various tasks to perform and kept a sharp eye on her. She then reached the conclusion that Anne was obedient, smart and willing to learn and work hard.

When Anne asked Marilla if she could stay at Green Gables, Marilla gave her one more task as a 'test', found fault with her work and made her rectify her mistake before telling her, 'Matthew and I have decided to keep you here.'

Anne started crying and said, 'I'm so glad! In fact, I'm more than glad! I'll do my best to be good.'

Marilla told her, 'Now calm down. You will need to go to school, but that will be in September since it is almost holiday time anyway.'

'What should I call you?' asked Anne. 'Miss Cuthbert? Or Aunt Marilla?'

'Just call me just Marilla.'

'Marilla,' Anne said in a demanding tone, 'Shall I find a close friend in Avonlea?'

The elder lady replied, 'There's Diana Barry who's your age. She lives at Orchard Slope. Right now, she's at Carmody, visiting her aunt. But you'll have to be careful. Mrs Barry is very strict.'

***

A fortnight after Anne arrived at Green Gables, Mrs Lynde arrived to have a look at her. She was full of curiosity about the orphan that Marilla and Matthew had taken on, about whom all kinds of stories had been circulating in Avonlea.

'I came here after I heard a few surprising things about Matthew and you,' Mrs Lynde said.

Marilla said, 'I've got over my surprise.'

Mrs Lynde said sympathetically, 'Could you not have sent her back?'

'We could have, but we decided against it; Matthew took a liking to her. I too liked her, despite her faults. Our house seems different already. She's a bright child.'

Mrs Lynde said gloomily, 'You've taken on a big responsibility. But I wouldn't want to dishearten you, Marilla.'

'I'm not discouraged,' Marilla replied quickly, 'I'll call Anne in.'

Anne's face was glowing with the beautiful things she had seen in the orchard but she halted in confusion at the door on seeing a stranger.

'They didn't select you for your appearance for sure,' Mrs Lynde commented emphatically. Apparently she prided herself on speaking frankly and continued, 'She's very skinny, Marilla. Come here, Anne, let me look closely at you. Such freckles! Your hair is red like carrots!'

Anne came, but in a way that Mrs Lynde least expected! The child bounded across the floor and stood in front of Mrs Lynde, her face red with anger, her lips trembling and her slender body quivering from head to toe.

'I hate you, I hate you, I hate you,' Anne cried out, stomping her foot louder each time she uttered the phrase.

'How dare you refer to me as ugly and skinny? How can you say that I'm freckled and a redhead? You are an impolite, rude and unfeeling woman!'

Marilla said, 'Anne!'

But Anne was firm.

'How would you feel if I told you that you are clumsy and fat! And probably don't have any imagination? I hope I have hurt your feelings. You have injured mine in a manner far worse than they have ever been by Mrs Thomas' drunk husband. I'll never forgive you for it!'

And Anne stomped her feet louder and louder.

'What a temper!' a horrified Mrs Lynde said.

Marilla told Anne to go to her room when she recovered her powers of speech.

To Mrs Lynde she said, 'You should not have teased her about her appearance, Rachel.'

Mrs Lynde was angry, 'Marilla Cuthbert, do you mean to say that you are backing her?'

'I'm not making excuses for her,' Marilla said slowly. 'She has been very naughty and I'll give her a dressing down. But one can't deny that you were a bit harsh on her, Rachel.'

'I'll give you some advice. When you scold that child, be sure you have a birch stick in your hand! That language would be most effective for a child like that.' With these words, Mrs Rachel Lynde swept out of the house.

Marilla walked slowly up the stairs and found Anne lying on her bed. She had to talk rather harshly to rouse her. Then, she told the child, 'You will have to apologize to Mrs Lynde.'

Anne said defiantly, 'I shall never, even if you put me in a dungeon with snakes and toads! How would you feel if someone told you that you were thin and ugly?'

Marilla recalled a time when she was a child, when one of her aunts had said to another, 'What a pity she is so homely and dark!' It had taken Marilla almost fifty years to get over the pain caused by that remark.

'You said you'd try to be a good girl so we'd keep you on at Green Gables. It wasn't like that this evening,' Marilla flung a parting shot at Anne before leaving the room.

When Marilla told Matthew about the morning's happenings, Matthew appeared to take Anne's side, which angered Marilla. In the evening, when Marilla went to get the cows back from the field, Matthew went upstairs and met Anne. He managed to convince her that apologizing to Mrs Lynde was the best solution to this problem—and Anne agreed!

And so the next day, after the milking was done, Marilla and Anne walked down the road, the former looking triumphant and Anne appearing dejected.

When they reached Mrs Lynde's, not a word was spoken when Anne all of a sudden knelt down before the astounded Mrs Lynde and said, 'Mrs Lynde, I am very, very sorry,' in a trembling voice. 'I will never be able express all my grief, even if I used all the words in a dictionary. I behaved in a terrible manner; I've disgraced dear Marilla and Matthew. I'm a very ungrateful and wicked girl, I deserve severe punishment. Please Mrs Lynde, forgive me!'

Anne was sincere in her deep apology. Both Mrs Lynde Marilla recognized its ring of sincerity. But Marilla understood, sadly, that Anne was really enjoying this humiliation; the thoroughness of her degradation was fun to her!

'Get up, Anne,' Mrs Lynde said warmly. 'I do forgive you. I was a bit too harsh on you. But I'm too much of an outspoken person. Your hair is very red, but I once knew a red-head in school. Her hair turned to a very pretty auburn when she became a young woman. I won't be surprised if yours became auburn too.'

Anne sighed and said, 'Mrs Lynde! You have given me hope. I will look upon you as my benefactor. I could tolerate anything if my hair were to become a handsome auburn!'

'You made a good apology,' Marilla told Anne. 'I hope you won't have to make more apologies like this. Keep a hold on your temper.'

The two proceeded to walk back home. Just before they reached Green Gables, Anne all of a sudden came close to Marilla and put her soft hand into Marilla's hard palm.

A pleasant and warm feeling welled up in the older woman's heart—a thumping of motherhood she had perhaps missed.

A few days later, Marilla was showing three new dresses that she had bought for the girl. Anne looked at them and in reply to Marilla's query, Anne said, 'I'll imagine I like them.'

An offended Marilla said, 'What's the matter with the dresses? They are new and clean and neat!'

'They're not very pretty,' Anne unwillingly said. 'But I am grateful; only thing is I do like dresses with puffed up sleeves.'

Marilla took Anne to meet Diana Barry, a pretty girl with rosy cheeks and black hair and a merry expression. After a short introduction, Anne clasped Diana's hands and asked her if she could be her best friend.

Diana laughed and said, 'I guess so. I'm so glad you've come to live here. It will be great to have someone to play with.'

After they returned, Marilla said to herself, 'She played with Diana half an hour more than I permitted her, and now she's chatting with Matthew when she knows she has to do her work.' She turned to Anne.

'Anne!' she called. 'Come here right now, do you hear me?'

Anne came running and said, 'There's a Sunday School picnic the following week. Can I go?'

'You were supposed to return at two o'clock. Now it's three,' Marilla scolded the girl, but quickly told her, 'Yes, of course, you can go for the picnic.'

Marilla looked troubled on the day before the picnic.

'Anne,' she said to the child, 'have you seen my purple pin? I can't find it.'

'I saw it on the pin cushion, and I had a look at it. I pinned it on my dress only to see how I would look.'

'Do you remember where the pin is now?'

'I put it back on the desk', said Anne.

Marilla said strictly, 'The brooch is not on the desk.'

Marilla searched the desk and other likely places but could not find the pin. She was convinced that Anne had misplaced it. So she punished Anne by sending her up to her room.

Marilla continued her search till late evening and later told Matthew about it. Her brother was both puzzled and helpless.

Marilla said grimly, 'Anne will have to stay in her room till she confesses. Any way she'll have to be punished severely.'

When Anne was told that she couldn't go for the picnic she was shattered.

The next morning Anne told Marilla, 'I'll confess about the pin.'

'Ah!' Marilla said as she put down her breakfast tray. Her method had been a success.

Anne gave a lengthy explanation of how she loved the pin and so, after putting it on, she went to the woods and imagined she was Lady Cordelia.

She told her, 'When I was on the bridge I got an urge to wear the pin again and look at myself in the shining water—and the pin fell into the river!

'Anne, you are the wickedest girl I know!'

'Yes, I think I am,' agreed Anne without any condition. 'Now please punish me quickly so that I can go for the picnic.'

'No picnic for you—that's your punishment!'

Later, Marilla noticed a small tear in her black shawl. She decided to mend it immediately.

The shawl was lying in her trunk. As Marilla lifted the shawl out, the sunlight lit up something that sparkled. It was the pin, stuck on a thread of the shawl!

When Marilla confronted Anne with this latest development, the girl replied that she had 'confessed' so that she could go for the picnic.

Despite herself, Marilla laughed!

'Anne, I'll forgive you. Get ready to go for the picnic.'

'Isn't it late, Marilla?'

'No, it's just two o'clock. Go quickly, and you can catch up in an hour.'

***

Gilbert Blythe, the smartest and handsomest boy in class was back in school after visiting his cousins over in New Brunswick all summer. He tried to get Anne's attention and when she did not respond, called her 'Carrots'.

Anne returned the compliment by hitting him on the head with a slate! The teacher punished her for it, even after Gilbert bravely confessed to teasing her.

The teacher, Mr Phillips, said he would punish all those who came late to class, but when several students came late one day he singled out Anne and punished only her. Anne was furious and told Marilla that she would never return to school again. Marilla said that she could stay at home until she felt like returning to school.

A few days later, Marilla told Anne, 'I'm going to the Aid Society meeting at Carmody this afternoon, Anne. You can call Diana over for tea, if you wish.'

'How lovely!' Anne said, clasping her hands in delight.

Diana and Anne first went for a walk in the apple orchard, where Anne helped herself to some of the tastiest fruits.

When they returned to the house, Anne asked Diana whether she would drink some raspberry juice. Diana agreed. Anne had to search for it as it was at the back of the shelf.

'I won't have any for I'm stuffed with apples,' Anne said, as Diana sipped the juice.

'It's so delicious, Anne,' Diana said, and Anne told her to help herself to it.

Diana drank another glassful of juice and, after Anne insisted her, downed a third generous serving.

'It's the best juice I ever had,' said Diana.

Diana suddenly got up and looked unsteady on her feet.

'I'm sick,' she said, thickly. 'I have to go.'

'But you haven't had tea!' said Anne.

***

On Monday, Anne went to Mrs Lynde's on an errand—and returned very soon, crying bitterly.

'Why are you crying?' asked Marilla.

Looking tragic, Anne sat up and said, 'Mrs Lynde went to see Mrs Barry today and the latter told her that I got Diana drunk on Saturday!'

Marilla was amazed.

'Diana, drunk! What did you give her?'

'Only raspberry juice,' said Anne.

Marilla marched to the pantry and soon discovered why Diana had got drunk; and it wasn't Anne's fault. Marilla had poured some wine in the empty juice bottle, causing the mix-up.

'Since you're not to blame, go to Mrs Barry and explain everything,' said Marilla to the girl.

When Anne asked Marilla to go instead, the latter agreed thinking that that would be wiser.

Marilla returned, cursing Mrs Barry. She exclaimed, 'That unreasonable woman did not believe that it was all a mistake.'

Anne then went and apologized to Mrs Barry, but the latter refused to listen to her either and forbade Anne from meeting Diana.

***

When Anne decided to return to school, her schoolmates gave her a warm welcome. She had been sorely missed in the singing, games, dramatics and book-reading. Several of her friends gave her small gifts but from Diana she got nothing—except a short note telling her that her (Diana's) mother had forbidden her from talking to Anne even in school.

Anne and Gilbert made good progress and were promoted to the fifth class where they started studying Latin, French, geometry and algebra.

Once the Canadian prime minsister came on a tour to address his supporters in the town. Marilla went for the meeting leaving Anne at home with Matthew.

The two were chatting when Diana Barry rushed in looking quite distressed.

'Anne, come quick,' said Diana. 'Minnie May is sick with croup.' Minnie was Diana's three-year-old sister. Anne hurriedly put on her jacket and hood and told Diana not to cry.

'I know just what to do in such cases.'

Anne hurried to Diana's house and worked quickly and skilfully. Soon, Minnie was well and fast asleep. Anne had lots of experience with croup, having taken care of all those children in the past.

When the doctor came he was full of praise for Anne.

'She saved the baby's life,' he told the Barrys.

Later, when Marilla returned home after hearing the PM's speech, she told Anne, 'Mrs Barry was here. She said she wanted you to forgive her and come at once and see Diana who is down with a cold.'

Anne's mood soared. Mrs Barry greeted her with a kiss when she arrived at their house, and Diana was again her best friend!

At summer's end Diana had a party at her house, where all the Sunday School girls were invited. They played adventure games—climbing trees and hopping on one foot.

Anne climbed onto the roof, took a few unsteady steps and then came crashing down. She had broken her ankle!

During the seven weeks she was in bed, Marilla realized how close the bond between her and Anne had become. She took special care of the child, even though she did not show her feelings outwardly.

By the time Anne was fit again, Christmas was round the corner. A concert has been planned for the coming festival. Matthew, knowing that Anne liked dresses with puffed sleeves, even went out and purchased some for her. The concert was a big success. The girls also recited a poem. At one point, Anne had to pretend to be dead, and would get a 'Norse burial'. For this, she had to lie down in a flat-bottomed boat and drift down the pond. Unfortunately, there was a hole in the barge, and it started to sink.

'Dear God, please take the flat close to a bridge pile and I'll do the rest,' she prayed, keeping her eyes peeled. When the barge neared the bridge, she climbed onto one of the knotty stubs and hung on, waiting for someone to help her get back to dry land.

Just as she thought she really could not endure the pain in her arms and wrists another moment, she spotted Gilbert coming towards her in a boat.

'Anne Shirley! How on earth did you get there?' he exclaimed but without waiting for an answer, he pulled close to the pile and extended his hand and helped her into his little boat.

He took her to the shore, and before she could leave disrespectfully, asked if they could be friends. Anne had not forgiven him for his comments yet, even though he had apologized and told her he thought her hair was 'really pretty'. But she said no, and stomped off.

'All right!' Gilbert said angrily. 'I'll never ask you to be friends again, Anne Shirley. And I don't care either!'

Later, Anne felt a pang of regret for her answer.

***

For the next three years, Gilbert and Anne continued to come first in class. Then they took the entrance exam for the Queen's Academy. Anne was very nervous about the results, but she and Gilbert, once again, topped the entire class! Marilla and Matthew had never felt so happy in their entire lives!

When her studies at the academy ended, Anne won a scholarship that would allow her to go to college for four years. Gilbert won the gold medal, but decided to become a teacher since his parents could not afford to send him to college. Instead of silence and enmity, Anne and Gilbert now shared a friendly rivalry.

Then, all of a sudden, tragedy struck. Abbey Bank collapsed. Matthew had kept his life's savings there and not taken his money out, even when people said it was no longer safe. So he lost everything. As a result, he suffered a heart attack and died.

Marilla, too, had developed eye problems. Her doctor said she had to stop sewing, reading and crying—or she would be blind.

Anne decided to give up the scholarship and stay on at Green Gables to look after the house and Marilla. She told the older woman not to sell Green Gables as she had originally intended to, since Anne had decided to teach at Carmody School. Gilbert had already been assigned the

teaching post at Avonlea. However, when he heard about Anne and Marilla's plight, he asked the school authorities to give Anne the Avonlea job. He offered to teach at Carmody instead.

Overjoyed and as optimistic as always, Anne thanked Gilbert and shook his hand, marking the end of their five-year rivalry and the start of a close friendship.

Ivanhoe: A Romance

Walter Scott

In 1066, William, Duke of the French region of Normandy, conquered England, where our story is set. By the end of the twelfth century, when our story unfolds, four generations have passed, and William's descendant—Richard the Lion-Hearted—is king. However, Richard is mostly away from England fighting the Crusades, and his brother, the hated Prince John, occupies the throne. The French-speaking Norman nobility hold complete power in the land. They build castles all over England and thwart whatever resistance the Saxons—the original inhabitants of the region—give them.

***

In the beautiful land was set between the towns of Sheffield and Doncaster, there used to be a large forest that covered beautiful valleys and hills. It was the scene of many battles during the War of the Roses. This area was also home to a famous band of outlaws—gallant men whose meritorious deeds have been immortalized in song and prose. However, at the time of our story—during the end of King Richard I's reign—there was trouble in the land.

The king, captured while fighting in the Crusades, lay imprisoned in Austria, leaving Prince John to rule in his place. The people spent their days desperately hoping for their king's return.

Norman noblemen had become all-powerful under Prince John's rule and abused their authority at will. They strengthened their castles, took away Saxon lands and turned Saxon landowners into serfs. As a result, the Saxon nobility was furious, and no one more so than the fiery Cedric of Rotherwood. He was so firmly anti-Norman, that he disinherited his son Ivanhoe for following Richard into battle. Moreover, Ivanhoe had fallen in love with his father's ward Rowena. Cedric had planned on marrying Rowena to Athelstane, a descendent of a long-dead Saxon king, thus re-establishing the Saxon line.

Our tale of adventure and bravery begins with two villagers, walking along a road and talking loudly about the origin of words like 'swine' and 'pork'. The older man looked savage and stern, and wore a sleeved jacket made of an animal's tanned skin with a little hair still left on it but which was quite worn out. His name was Gurth and he was a swineherd. Beside him was a man some ten years younger whose dress was similar to Gurth's, but a bit more fancier because of its bright colours. He was called Wamba, a clownish figure who had a cunning look on his face.

By and by, a group of horsemen galloped past them. Two of these horsemen stood out because they rode ahead of the others and wore distinguished clothes. One was dressed in the robes of a monk and rode a mule, while the other was a strong, slim and muscular man of at least forty years. His face and expression made him look fearsome and awe-inspiring. A deep scar on his brow and thick moustache made him look even more imposing. He rode on a pony while his guards led his warhorse behind him. The others had dark skins and wore white turbans and Oriental garments, marking them as being from an Eastern country from Asia.

Wamba recognized the monk. He was Prior Aymer.

'Is there anyone who could give us food and hospitality for one night?' he asked Wamba.

Wamba replied that the Brinxworth monastery a few miles away or they could go onto Copmanhurst, a hermitage, but the Prior rejected these proposals. He said he was seeking the residence of Cedric of Rotherwood, the Saxon, and asked if Wamba could show him how to get there.

Gurth broke his silence, 'It's a tough road to find'.

'Cedric's family goes to bed early,' Gurth added coldly.

Immediately, an argument broke out between Gurth and the strangers, mainly because of the proud manners of the Norman horsemen. But Prior Aymer was against any form of violence.

'Brother Brian', he addressed his companion, 'this is not Palestine and you are not fighting the Turks.'

Again, he asked Wamba the way to Cedric's. When Wamba complained about the Prior's companion, Aymer explained that Brian de Bois-Guilbert was a Knight Templar, a warrior-monk and was therefore quick-tempered.

As the Prior and the Templar rode on, they met a palmer—a holy man who wore palm leaves as a sign of having visited the Holy Land—who directed the group to Cedric's castle. This palmer accompanied them from there.

***

Cedric the Saxon was preparing for his evening meal in the great hall of his castle. On the dais were huge chairs made of carved oak while the walls were decorated with attractive curtains and hangings.

Cedric appeared to be a frank man, but one who had a short temper. He was broad-shouldered and of medium height. His arms were long and powerful like one who is used to the fatigues of battles or of the hunt. He had a broad face, big blue eyes and a fine set of teeth. His head was well-formed and he looked to be approaching the age of sixty. He was dressed in a forest green tunic and he wore sandals that were similar to those of the peasants, except that his were made of finer materials. There were several servants in the hall.

Cedric was not in a peaceful state of mind. His ward, Lady Rowena, had just returned from attending service at a distant church, and was at that moment changing her clothes which had been ruined by a storm.

There was no news about Gurth and his companion. This was important to Cedric, since the income of Saxon landlords often depended on the state of their large herds of swine. Besides, Cedric also missed Wamba, his favourite clown. Suddenly, there was noise at the gates.

A guard came into Cedric's hall and announced, 'Prior Aymer of Jorvaulx—who is travelling with Brian de Bois-Guilbert, commander of the order of the Knights Templar, and a small group—has asked for lodging and hospitality. They are en route to a horseback fighting tournament at Ashby-de-la-Zouche.'

Cedric replied, 'They are Normans but we will welcome them here.'

He told one of his servants to take care of the guests, their mules and horses and ensure that they lacked nothing. Cedric also told his servant to tell them that he could, under oath, walk only three steps from the dais to meet people who did not share royal Saxon blood.

The Prior and the Knight Templar changed into fine clothes before coming to the dining table. They looked handsome in their elegant clothes and fine ornaments.

The palmer wore a cloak of coarse sacking cloth. His sandals too were coarse and were tied with strings. He wore a big, broad hat and on his long iron staff was the branch of a palm.

Before the feast started, Rowena entered with her female attendants and was escorted to her appointed place beside Cedric.

The eyes of Brian de Bois-Guilbert were glued to Rowena for this tall, fair Saxon beauty appeared more elegant than all the Eastern ladies he had seen. She had blue eyes and long hair arranged in many ringlets. Rowena did not like the way the Knight Templar looked at her and covered her face with her veil, in such a manner that clearly showed her dislike for the Templar.

The conversation between Cedric and his guests led to the revelation that his visitors were on their way to the tournament—when suddenly they heard someone at the gates. The servant who went out to see who it was returned to say that it was a tall, thin Jew named Isaac and asked whether he should be admitted. Cedric said yes and Isaac was given a seat at the lower end of the table. He wore a plain russet coat, big boots and a small knife. As Jews were generally not well-treated in those days, no one paid the newcomer much attention.

The conversation turned towards the might of English warriors versus those of the French. Lady Rowena wondered why no Englishman was mentioned in the same breath as the Knight Templar.

Brian de Bois-Guilbert answered that English warriors—as he had seen in Palestine—were inferior. At once, the palmer took offence. Unexpectedly, he exclaimed that English warriors were second to nobody and their courage was unquestioned. He went on to relate events in the Holy Land where English soldiers had stood out.

The conversation continued on the lines of who the best warriors were. The palmer listed the top five—all Englishmen—and said that the sixth best knight was a young and renowned man of lower rank.

De Bois-Guilbert scoffed at this, and declared that he knew the name of this knight.

'It is the Knight of Ivanhoe', he said, adding that if Ivanhoe were in England, he, de Bois-Guilbert, would challenge him at the tournament. To this, the palmer replied, 'If Ivanhoe comes back from Palestine, I will ensure that he meets you.'

As a pledge to his promise, the palmer handed the Templar a relic of the cross on which Jesus Christ was crucified, which he had brought from Palestine.

Lady Rowena then asked her attendants to leave her and spoke alone to the palmer. She asked him about Ivanhoe. The palmer said that he did not know much about that knight, but knew that he had survived the mistreatment meted out to him by his enemies in Palestine and was about to return to England.

Later, the palmer was given a rough bed, which he slept on. The next morning, the palmer saw Isaac lying on another similarly rough bed in the same room. He quickly woke him by poking his staff into his side and told him to leave the place at once for he had heard the Templar tell his slaves to arrest the Jew.

This information shocked Isaac so much that he trembled. He was worried as to how he would escape without being caught. But the palmer helped him. He told Gurth to open the back gate so that he could escort the Jew out of there. When Gurth seemed unhappy at carrying out this task, the palmer whispered something in his ear. This did the trick. Not only did Gurth quickly get up, open the gate, and see them off on two mules that Wamba brought, he also kissed the palmer's hand respectfully. As they left, Isaac hid something in his clothing. His behaviour indicated that he was carrying something of value.

After some time, the palmer told Isaac that they had to part ways. However, the Jew said that he would help the palmer get armour and a horse. He then scribbled a note and gave it to the palmer and told him to take it to a rich Jew, who would give him all that he needed.

***

In the meantime, Prince John, along with Philip of France—King Richard's worst enemy—was trying to influence the Duke of Austria to keep his brother imprisoned for a longer time. John was in the process of strengthening his own forces, which he hoped to use to gain the throne permanently.

A band of outlaws had been driven to the forest, in despair of the oppressive feudal nobility. They held onto the forest lands and challenged the country's magistracy and justice system. There were other bands of thieves too, created by the nobles to carry out their dirty work. To retain these outlaws, the nobles borrowed heavily from the Jews at high rates of interest. Consequently, it was the citizens of England who suffered the most. To provide them with some entertainment, a grand sporting spectacle—called the Passage of Arms—was going to be held at Ashby in Leicester. People of all ranks were expected to attend, and Prince John was to be the guest of honour.

At the central pavilion in Ashby, Brian de Bois-Guilbert was given the place of honour, due to his fame in such sports and his contacts with the knights of the tournament. Then there were tents for John's friends—Richard de Malvoisin and Reginald Front-de-Boeuf, and for noblemen of the area, Hugh de Grantmesnil and William Rufus, his son. A knight of St John of Jerusalem, Ralph de Vipont, was in the fifth pavilion.

Spectators from all walks of life jammed the arena. Two marshals, Stephen de Martival and William de Wyvil, rode by to ensure order among the fans, as the galleries were soon filled with nobles and knights—all dressed up for the occasion—along with their richly adorned ladies.

Isaac arrived at the pavilion and tried to make some place for his daughter, a beautiful girl named Rebecca.

Prince John had been negotiating for a huge loan from the Jews of the city of York. Isaac had a considerable share in this deal and he was confident that Prince John would protect him if the transaction were completed quickly.

Prince John himself was mounted on a fine warhorse and majestically dressed in gold and in crimson. He had a falcon on his hand and his head was covered by a fur bonnet, ornamented with precious stones. His curled hair spread on his shoulders. His sharp eye immediately recognized Isaac. However, he was far more attracted to Rebecca, the Jew's lovely daughter who hung on to her old father's arm.

Rebecca was as beautiful as any proud English lady. She was dressed in exquisite Eastern clothing. She had brilliant eyes, a nicely-formed nose, pearl white teeth and a crop of luxuriant hair. A diamond necklace was strung around her beautiful neck.

'Is she your daughter or wife?' Prince John asked Isaac.

'Rebecca, is my daughter,' the old man replied.

John did not address Cedric the Saxon and his group, among whom sat Athelstane of Coningsburgh. As he had descended from Saxon monarchs, Athelstane was highly respected by the Saxons of northern England. But Athelstane was a strong, heavy-browed, dull-eyed and slow person who was referred to as Athelstane the Unready. John behaved badly when he asked him to make way for Rebecca and Isaac. But Athelstane refused to obey the Prince's command. So John

told one of his advisors, Maurice De Bracy to poke the Saxon with his rod. Just as De Bracy was about to do that, Cedric pulled out a short sword and cut off the tip of De Bracy's rod.

One of the contestants fought under the title of the 'Disinherited Knight'. He was of medium size and looked more thinner than strong. His steel armour was richly adorned with gold and on his shield was a device that had the word 'Desdichado', meaning 'Disinherited' in Spanish. He rode a handsome black horse. His talent with the horse and a youthful grace made him the favourite of the crowd at the arena.

On the contest's opening day he made a dramatic entry, challenged de Bois-Guilbert and stole the show by defeating all his rivals—including de Bois-Guilbert. After a great series of victories on Day One, the Disinherited Knight was given the honour of selecting the Queen of Love and Beauty—the lady who would crown the victor at the end of the tournament—for the tournament's competition the next day.

When the mysterious knight chose Rowena's as his Queen of Love and Beauty, the Normans were shocked. The knight had another surprise for them: he declined to attend the banquet held by Prince John to celebrate the first day's competition.

The Disinherited Knight fought de Bois-Guilbert, Reginald Front-de-Boeuf and Athelstane and Reginald Front-de-Boeuf on the second day of the tournament. The knight fought bravely and—helped by a mysterious fighter called the Black Knight—defeated both de-Bouef and Athelstane. He charged de Bois-Guilbert and unhorsed him, thus winning the championship in great fashion. When Rowena stepped out to crown the victor, she removed his helmet and the Disinherited Knight was revealed to be the palmer. Everyone was shocked to find that the palmer had been Ivanhoe all along!

Ivanhoe had won, but he was so badly wounded, he lost consciousness and fell at Rowena's feet.

The news of Ivanhoe's identity quickly spread among the crowd and Prince John had hurried discussions with his advisors.

The Prince had assumed Ivanhoe to be dead and had promised to give Ivanhoe's castle to Sir Reginald Front-de-Boeuf, and was now faced with a dilemma. He suggested that his personal doctor 'see' Ivanhoe—implying that the returning knight could be killed. However, Ivanhoe's friends took good care of him and nursed him back to health.

Meanwhile, John's ambitions hit another obstruction. He received a message that read: 'Take care, the Devil has been unchained.' John assumed this meant that King Richard was returning to England, and he panicked. John and his henchmen decided to quickly finish the tournament—and then gather the support they would badly need when Richard returned.

The archery competition the next day was won by the gallant Locksley—who was actually the famous outlaw Robin Hood. He comfortably beat the king's champion, Hubert.

John then decided on another ploy to get support. He invited the Saxon nobility to a banquet that he held that night. But at the feast, tensions arose between the Normans and the Saxons. To soothe things, John passed around a wine glass, asking the two groups to drink to each other's good health. Cedric had already refused to drink to Ivanhoe, or even recognize him as his son. He had still not forgiven Ivanhoe for fighting in the Crusades and being loyal to the Norman King Richard. Now, he declared that, in his opinion, King Richard was the only Worthy Norman. John became white in the face on hearing Cedric's praise of Richard, but could do nothing except drink to the brother whose very name he hated.

Meanwhile, De Bracy had fallen madly in love with Rowena. John had planned for them to get married but the impatient De Bracy intended to kidnap her entire party.

When the Saxons started to ride back home from the banquet, they met Rebecca and Isaac who sought their protection. On Rowena's plea, Cedric agreed to take care of them and the party went on its way, when suddenly they were attacked by De Bracy and his henchmen who had disguised themselves as forest outlaws.

Wamba managed to escape but the remaining Saxons, along with Rebecca and Isaac were captured. Deep in the forest, Wamba came face-to-face with Locksley, the real forest outlaw. Though he was an outlaw, Locksley led an honourable band of men. He took Wamba and Gurth to the chapel of a friar who was giving company to the Black Knight. After the tournament, the Knight had found a hermitage in the forest and had made friends with the friar. The knight and the priest agreed to lend a hand in rescuing the prisoners.

De Bracy's men hauled off the prisoners to Reginald Front-de-Boeuf's castle, where Isaac was flung into a dungeon and handed an ultimatum: give Front-de-Boeuf one thousand pieces of silver or be painfully tortured. Isaac asked that Rebecca be allowed to go to York to get the money, but was told that Rebecca was now the property of Sir Brian de Bois-Guilbert. De-Boeuf's slaves ripped Isaac's clothes and readied him for torture. But these grim proceedings were halted when a bugle sounded at the gates. Soon, they heard voices anxiously looking for de-Bouef.

While the threat of torture was hanging over Isaac's head, Rowena was imprisoned somewhere else. De Bracy was stubborn in his intent to marry her and threatened to kill Ivanhoe and his father Cedric. Rowena was unaware that Ivanhoe too was being held captive by De Bracy and she started to cry. De Bracy was moved by this and attempted awkwardly to pacify her. Then he heard the bugle blow and rushed out of the chamber.

In the same castle, in another prison, Rebecca was imprisoned along with a miserable Saxon named Ulrica. De Bois-Guilbert told Rebecca that she belonged to him and made a move to grab her. When Rebecca threatened to jump off

the castle wall if he did not step back, de Bois was impressed and tried to placate her. De Bois-Guilbert too rushed from the room when he heard the bugle.

The sound of the bugle heralded the delivery of a letter that bore Wamba's and Gurth's signatures, but was written by the Black Knight and Locksley. It declared that its writers intended to free the prisoners by combat or by siege. Front-de-Boeuf delivered a message to the visitors which sought a priest who would hear the prisoners' final confessions. Actually, De-Boeuf's plan was to send the priest to get reinforcements, for 200 archers had surrounded the castle. Wamba wore the gown of a priest and quietly entered the castle and changed his clothing with Cedric's.

The disguised Cedric roamed around the castle halls, where he met Rebecca who was taking care of the injured Ivanhoe. He also met Ulrica the Saxon, who told him her life story. She explained that after the Normans seized the castle from her ancestors, she befriended them to protect her life. Then, when she became old and lost her beauty, they began to hate her and threw her into the dungeon.

Cedric then approached de-Boeuf, who gave him a letter for de-Boeuf's ally, Philip Malvoisin. De-Boeuf also gave him a gold coin for his troubles. Cedric was greatly angered by this and flung the coin back before hurrying away from the castle. When the Normans realized what had happened, they prepared for a battle with the outlaws.

Rebecca continued taking care of Ivanhoe, even after the battle began. She stood at the window and described the ongoing fighting to him. Rebecca was shocked by all the bloodshed and criticized the system of knighthood, but Ivanhoe defended chivalry and said it was a code of morality and honour. Exhausted, Ivanhoe again became unconscious. Rebecca was falling in love with Ivanhoe, and tried hard not to show it.

De-Boeuf led the castle's defenders against the Black Knight and Locksley's archers. When he got fatally wounded and slumped over, Ulrica teased him. A mad Ulrica then set fire to the castle; the flames spread in the hallways. The Black Knight captured De Bracy and then bravely charged into the castle to rescue Ivanhoe from the fire. The other prisoners escaped by themselves but, amid the smoke, Rebecca was captured by de Bois-Guilbert. Athelstane tried to stop the Templar but the latter dealt a heavy blow to his head. The huge wall of the castle then got engulfed in fire, which consumed both Ulrica and De-Bouf.

The Saxons, along with the band of liberators, met at Locksley's 'home' in the forest. There, Cedric granted Gurth his freedom. When the booty taken from the castle was split up, the Black Knight took what was due to him but the proud Cedric refused to accept any share of the Norman's wealth. The Black Knight also freed De Bracy.

The friar too arrived at the spot with Isaac, who became dejected when he learned that Rebecca had been kidnapped. Prior Aymer said he would write to the Templar, asking for the girl's release. As Isaac started off for the Knights Templars' bastion armed with the Prior's letter, the Saxons said goodbye to Locksley and his men and got ready for the difficult job of taking Athelstane's body back to his castle.

In the meanwhile De Bracy rushed to Prince John and told him that Richard was back in England. De Bracy also told the Prince that De-Boeuf had died, and that de Bois-Guilbert had abducted Rebecca. John was startled, but soon invented a plan to attack Richard and imprison him. Prince John did not intend to give up the English throne!

Isaac travelled to Templar headquarters in Templestowe and showed the Prior's letter to the knights' Grand Master, Lucas Beaumanoir.

The letter put the honour of Bois-Guilbert at stake by stating that he was keeping a Jewlady at Templestowe. It also suggested that Rebecca had cast a spell on the Templar to induce him to love her. Albert Malvoisin, the ruler of Templestowe, added that Rebecca's witchcraft was more to blame for her being at Templestowe than de Bois-Guilbert's weakness. Malvoisin sternly lectured de Bois-Guilbert on his incorrect ways. He said Rebecca should suffer like a witch. De Bois-Guilbert was against this line of action but Malvoisin sarcastically told him that he had no say in the matter.

So Beaumanoir declared that Rebecca would be tried at once as a witch. Malvoisin did not actually believe that Rebecca was a witch; he just wanted to save de Bois-Guilbert's reputation within the order and so started searching for reasons to convict Rebecca and execute her.

Rebecca's trial began when the charges against de Bois-Guilbert were read—and summarily rejected on the grounds that Rebecca was to blame for the Templar's wrongdoings. Malvoisin brought in false witnesses, who testified that Rebecca had supernatural healing powers. They also accused her of other strange things.

Certain that she would be found guilty, de Bois-Guilbert asked her to seek a trial by combat.

When she agreed to this, the Templars sent a message to Isaac asking him to find a champion to fight for her at the trial by combat. De Bois-Guilbert felt that no one would step forward because knights would not fight for Jews. So he asked her to run away with him.

Meanwhile, the Black Knight and Wamba travelled in the forest, exchanging jokes, songs and riddles. Ivanhoe told the Prior that he wanted permission to follow the two and when he got it, Ivanhoe set out after borrowing the Prior own horse.

Elsewhere, arrows suddenly whizzed by the Black Knight and Wamba. They were being attacked by men led by Prince John's councillor, Waldemar Fitzurse. Helped by Locksley's men, the Knight and Wamba overpowered their attackers. Fitzurse then referred to the Black Knight as 'Richard'—after which the Black Knight removed his helmet and revealed himself as King Richard, who was eventually back in England. Richard ordered Fitzurse to be banished from the land but spared Prince John of guilt for the attack. As the group was getting ready to move on, two men on horses approached them. They were Gurth and Ivanhoe.

Richard then told Ivanhoe that all his men were now aware of his identity. Ivanhoe warned the king against going abroad on silly adventures when he was sorely needed in his own country.

Richard replied he could not yet, for some reasons, tell the nation who he truly was. He said he was waiting for his allies to get together a strong army to fight John. They all had a feast at Robin Hood's camp—Locksley had also revealed his identity by then. After the feast, they rushed to Coningsburgh Castle to attend Athelstane's funeral.

When they reached the castle, the group was shocked to see Athelstane himself greet them. He said that de Bois-Guilbert seemingly fatal blow had only put him into a coma. He was now fully recovered. He then urged Cedric to give Rowena to Ivanhoe in marriage, stating that he was not worthy of her. Athelstane wanted to join Ivanhoe's hand with Rowena's, but the party could not find Ivanhoe or Richard. They had both disappeared.

Meanwhile, a huge crowd had gathered at Templestowe to witness Rebecca's trial by combat. Against his wishes, De Bois-Guilbert had been made the Templars' champion. This meant that he would face Rebecca's champion—if she got one.

Even as de Bois-Guilbert lost his patience and rode his horse up and down as time passed, Ivanhoe charged in to Rebecca's defence. He attacked de Bois-Guilbert who had to defend for even if he won the trial, Rebecca would be executed. An exhausted Ivanhoe fell from his horse at the first pass, but de Bois-Guilbert too tumbled to the ground—and died, his conflicting passions bringing about his death.

Ivanhoe and Rowena got married, and Rebecca visited Rowena to congratulate her and thank her for Ivanhoe's role in saving her life. She and her father planned to leave England forever. Ivanhoe went on to distinguish himself while serving King Richard, but his services were no longer needed when the king was killed in a battle near Limoges.

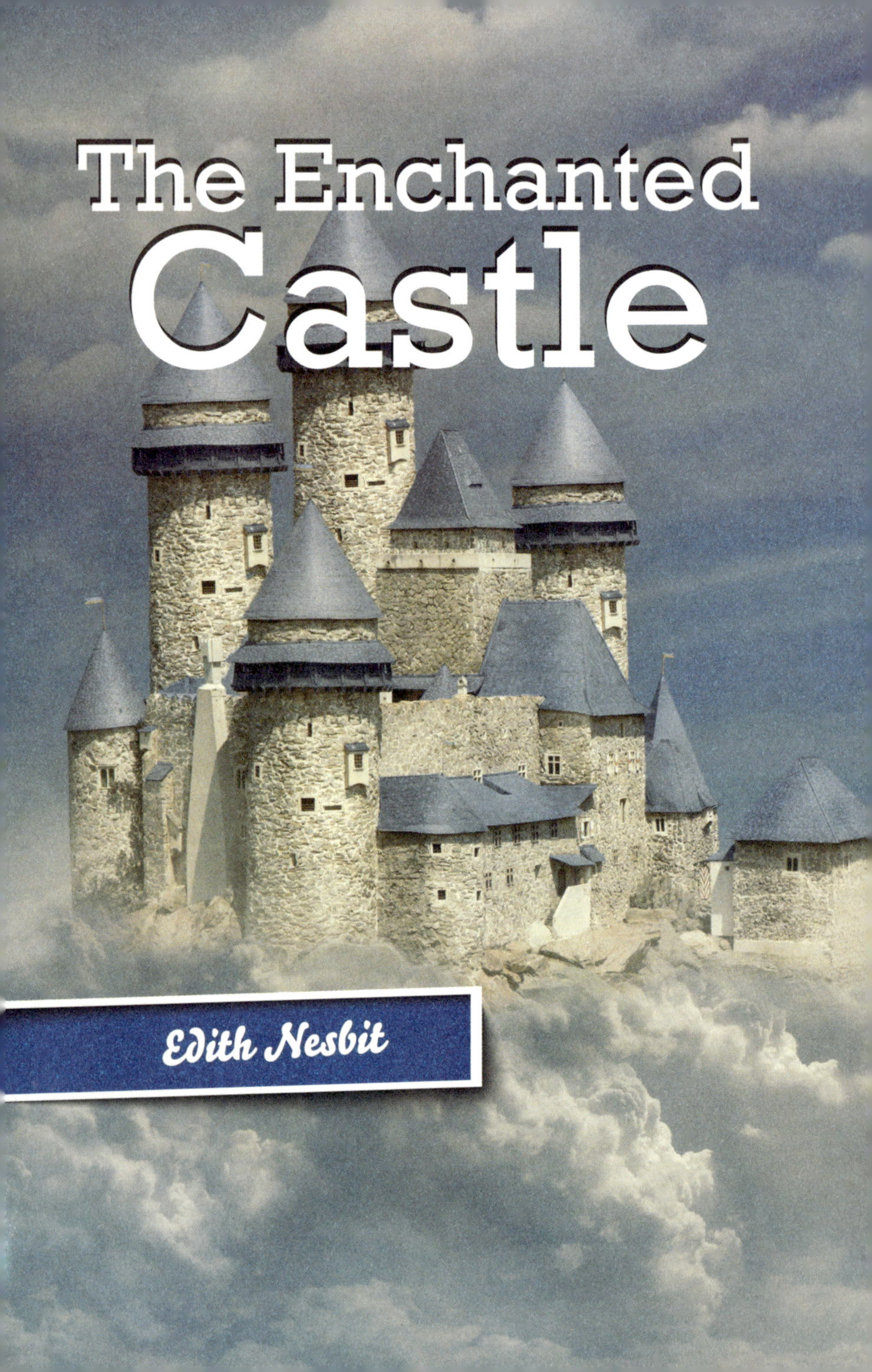
The Enchanted Castle
Edith Nesbit

Jerry and Jimmy studied in a different boarding school from their sister Kathleen—who was usually called Cathy. So they were always excited to play together at home during the holidays. This year, however, their cousin Betty (who was supposed to be spending the summer with them) came down with measles. So the three siblings were forced to spend the summer in Cathy's school. All the girls had gone home, and only the French mistress remained. The very first day after the boys—whose real names were Gerald and James, respectively—came to Cathy's school, the siblings went out exploring. They soon got lost, and accidentally discovered a secret cave. Naturally, they had to explore it! The cave ended in a passage that led to a tree-lined path, and a marble terrace which glimmered in the sunlight. Below that was a lake, with an island in the middle! In the distance, white marble statues shone among the trees. There was also a round, white, pillared building and a waterfall!

'It is a magic castle,' said Cathy.

Then, the children came to a maze. After failing thrice to reach the centre, they almost gave up and went back to get their food. However, Jimmy noticed a red rose near the yew hedge.

Announcing it was a magical clue, Jerry followed the thread to the maze's centre, where they found a low marble seat. When they went closer they found the statue of a girl on it.

'Sleeping Beauty!' exclaimed Kathleen and added, 'Jerry you're the prince. You have to wake her with a kiss!'

When Jerry refused, little Jimmy planted a cheerful-sounding kiss on the princess's cheek. She opened big, dark eyes, and stretched a bit.

'Are you a princess?' Jimmy asked her.

'Of course,' she answered, and invited them to the castle.

After they had eaten a simple meal of bread and cheese, the princess said, 'Let's go and see my treasures.'

She led them to a small but high room with stars on the ceiling. It was also completely empty.

The princess then told the others to close their eyes and muttered a long, nonsensical word. When they opened their eyes, the room was filled with the most glorious treasures, displayed against velvet blue!

'All these things are magical!' the princess exclaimed, showing them a magic ring.

Jerry asked if she could grant wishes. She said no, but offered to show them how the ring made her invisible.

'Shut your eyes and count to fifty!'

They did as she said. When they opened their eyes again, she had disappeared and so had the jewels!

'That surely is magic,' exclaimed Cathy.

'Now, shut your eyes again and count to fifty,' the princess' voice said.

Cathy and Jerry closed their eyes, but Jimmy forgot. He saw her hiding under a panel near the window. Then Jimmy remembered and closed his eyes. They all counted to fifty—but the princess did not reappear!

She had really turned invisible, but no one believed that—not even the invisible princess. She thought the others were pretending not to see her, and they thought she was hiding. So she pushed Jerry, and the children realized the truth. So then they dragged the princess to a mirror. She could not see her reflection and began to cry.

'It was all a game. I cannot do any magic... There's a hidden panel which opens up the "treasures" and when you closed your eyes, I hid in a secret chamber!' she said, adding, 'My name is Mabel Prowse and my aunt is the castle's housekeeper.'

Mabel was also surprised because the magic ring did make her invisible. She wrote a note for her aunt, stating that a lady had adopted her. She also mentioned that they were going to travel in a ship and that the aunt should not worry about her. Then Mabel decided to stay with her new friends.

The next morning, the children went to a fair, where Jerry disguised himself as an Indian magician and earned some money by doing 'disappearing' tricks. Of course, everything that disappeared went straight into the invisible Mabel's pocket!

After the show, Mabel managed to remove the ring and became visible again. A few moments later, Jerry put on the ring, and disappeared. He could not get it off either!

The children wondered how to explain Jerry's absence and Mabel's presence to Mademoiselle, the French teacher in Cathy's school, under whose care the children were staying.

'Ask Mademoiselle to allow Mabel to stay the night, since it's too late for her to go home,' Jerry suggested mockingly, 'and you could tell her I've gone to bed with a headache.'

'If I was invisible, I wouldn't waste it by going to bed early,' Jimmy sulked. 'I'd be a detective.'

'That's a great idea! I'll do that!' Jerry cried.

'There's got to be something to detect before you can begin detectiving,' Mabel pointed out.

So they went to the police station, where they saw a poster that offered a fifty-pound reward to anyone who could help recover some silver that had been stolen from Houghton Grange.

'I'll detect that burglary,' Jerry decided.

Since he was invisible, Jerry told Jimmy what to ask Constable Johnson. Johnson said he knew exactly who had stolen the silver but could not arrest the man since he had no evidence.

The children thanked the constable and were leaving, when Mabel remembered that they had left the window to the treasure room open, with the key inside.

'Perfect!' Jerry jumped in. 'I'll climb in at the window, shut the window, put the key back in its place, and slip out unnoticed.'

He told Cathy to leave a window open for him, and took off running with Mabel. When Jerry dropped Mabel off at home, her aunt hugged her and said, 'Oh, Mabel, thank heaven you're safe!'

As Jerry went ahead, alone and invisible, he saw a white creature emerge from among the trees. He soon realized that all the statues had come alive, as a life-sized stone dinosaur walked by. He was not afraid, until he reached out a hand and touched it. Then, he fled towards the house in terror.

When he had recovered Jerry saw the stone dinosaur was indulging in the fish-pool. Then, he went in, shut the window, opened the door, went out, locked the door again, hung the key on its usual nail and crept to the end of the passage.

By now, Jerry was very hungry. While looking for the kitchen, he came to a door with a light under it. Reminding himself to be brave, Jerry opened the door, and found three men stealing some silver! Jerry could not wait to get back and tell the gang that he had discovered a burglary on his very first night as a detective. He needed help, but who could he ask? He thought for a while, and then wrote a note. It said: 'Burglars in the strong room. Call police. I will follow the burglars if they leave before the police arrive.'

He signed it, 'From a friend,' tied it to a stone with a shoelace, and threw it into the room where Mabel and her aunt were celebrating their reunion with a feast. Mabel realized it was Jerry, and begged her aunt to wake Bates, the gardener, to fetch the police. By the time the police came, most of the silver was gone.

When Eliza, the maid, came to wake Jerry the next morning, she found a dirty, empty bed. Then, she looked away and looked back to find Jerry lying in bed.

Her scream woke Jimmy.

'How did you get visible?' he asked.

'It just happened when Eliza called me and the ring came off.'

'Where's the ring?' Jimmy asked after breakfast. 'I want to try it now.'

'I forgot it,' said Jerry. 'It must be in the bed somewhere.'

But it was not, and Eliza—who had made the bed—swore she had not seen any ring.

***

Jerry dragged his siblings out, saying he had other plans. When he told them of his adventures, Cathy and Jimmy listened open-mouthed. He was nearing the end of the story, when Mabel met them and asked what she had missed.

Jerry replied, 'When I got back to the castle from your house, the burglars were still there. When they left, I followed them to their hideout.'

He then told them about the statues coming to life. Mabel replied that maybe the ring allowed him to see them alive.

'Ok, now run, we're late,' Jerry cried, and led them all to Constable Johnson's house.

There, he told the policeman how and where to catch the thieves.

Later after lunch, Mabel said, 'We should put

the ring back. Where is it?'

Cathy told Mabel the ring had missing, but Mabel wanted to look for it by herself. By this time, Eliza had left to meet her fiancé.

About ten minutes later, just as Mabel came down the stairs empty-handed, she was walking helplessly as though dragged by an invisible person.

Eliza had found the ring, put it on, and become invisible. The children understood immediately.

'If I'd stolen a ring,' said Jerry, 'I would go indoors and be quiet.'

Eliza let go of the man, and went inside. The man regained some composure.

'You say your fiancée was holding your hand, but you couldn't see her. Well, Eliza's inside and cannot meet anyone today,' Mabel said.

'Why don't you go home and lie down? You'll feel better tomorrow,' Jerry added politely.

The man left and the children went inside. There, Eliza was crying.

'I didn't steal the ring. I just wanted to borrow it, since I was going to meet Elf,' she said, as tears rolled off her invisible nose. 'But why did he say he couldn't see me?'

When the children showed her that she really was invisible, Eliza fainted. The children revived her and explained that she can never be sure what will happen if she stole—or even borrowed—a ring.

Then, the children decided to take her out on a tea-picnic to cheer her up. The children set the table for Mademoiselle's tea. Then, all left for Yalding Towers with some cakes.

As they were having their tea, Eliza pointed out a statue that had come alive. Like Jerry, she was also fearless, until she touched one of the statues. Then, she screamed and ran off. The children ran after her and reached their backdoor just as the church clock struck half past nine.

'Take off the ring. Perhaps it'll come off now,' Jerry said to thin air and suddenly Eliza was visible again.

The next day, both Elf and Eliza told themselves that they had dreamed the whole thing. Meanwhile, Constable Johnson had caught the criminals and become a hero.

The next day, the four children brought Mademoiselle some flowers. In return, she showed them a beautiful sketch of Yalding Towers that she had made. Mabel then said she lived at Yalding, and Mademoiselle seemed impressed.

But then Mabel clarified that she was the housekeeper's niece and that Lord Yalding did not live there because he was too poor. She told them how Lord Yalding's uncle had left all the money to some distant cousin as he did not approve of the lady Lord Yalding wanted to marry. Poor Lord Yalding had just enough to pay for all the maintenance. He could not even sell the house because of legal issues.

'It is nearly lunch-time,' Mademoiselle announced, 'I shall go and get some cakes, and we shall have a feast.'

As the children waited, Jerry pointed out that Mabel had been invisible for twenty-one hours, he for fourteen, and Eliza for seven.

'Maybe it won't turn you invisible anymore,' he said.

Soon, Mademoiselle returned with treats—plums, grapes, jam tarts, soda, raspberry vinegar and chocolates—and a big bunch of roses, which she used to make garlands for them. She even persuaded Jimmy to wear one, saying that Greek gods and goddesses always wore garlands at a feast.

After lunch, Jerry asked if she liked acting and plays. When she said yes, the children promised to act a play for her and Eliza that evening.

When it was time for the performance to start, Mademoiselle and Eliza were startled to find half a dozen chairs already occupied. It was the strangest audience—an old woman with a bonnet, a lady in a large straw hat and several men with strange, clumsy figures, all with hats on.

These were the children's Ugly-Wuglies, with bodies of bolsters and rolled-up blankets, broom-handles, hockey sticks, umbrellas and wooden hangers; their faces were paper masks that Jerry had painted (quite badly) that afternoon.

The play, *Beauty and the Beast*, charmed the audience. When the curtains fell, two people clapped warmly. The Beast (Jerry) had given Beauty (Mabel) the ring during the play, and she had jokingly wished that their fake audience had been alive. Well, now they were. The magic ring had turned into a wishing ring!

Jerry tried to wish that the Ugly-Wuglies were not alive but that did not work.

Soon, a pointed white face with red cheeks looked up at him, and wide red lips said, 'Aa 00 re o me me oo a oo ho el'

It was repeated four times, before Jerry realized the scary creature was saying—very politely—'Can you recommend me a good hotel?'

Jerry's heart sank. Yet, he managed to politely say, 'I'm awfully sorry but all our hotels shut early. And they're all run by deaf people. So we can't even knock on the door!'

He led the Ugly-Wuglies out to the yard, and quickly stepped back into the house to reassure Jimmy and the girls—who were terrified—and convince Mademoiselle that it was all just a trick. He then said he was taking Mabel home and the two left by the front door.

It took all of Mabel's nerve not to turn around and run away screaming when Jerry introduced her to the six Ugly-Wuglies. Jerry's plan was to lock the Ugly-Wuglies inside a secret passage behind the Temple of Flora near the maze at Yalding Towers and leave them there until they were not alive anymore. When they got there, the Ugly-Wuglies were delighted with the place!

Mabel pressed a secret spring on the Temple's walls and a large stone revolved slowly to reveal a high and narrow doorway.

Jerry gave the lantern to the oldest Ugly-Wugly, who led the others all into the passage. The children held their breath until the last Ugly-Wugly had gone a little way inside. Then, they let out a sob of relief and tried to close the door. Suddenly, the Ugly-Wuglies realized what was happening, and fought fiercely to open it again. As the children struggled, they heard a man's voice.

'What's up, there?' it cried.

'Come and help push!' Jerry yelled. 'If they get out, they'll kill us all.'

Soon, a strong shoulder joined in the effort, and the door clicked shut.

Then, the man sat down with the children and told them he was a bailiff who had come to take care of Yalding Towers. He wanted the children to tell him the entire story. Jerry realized they would have to tell him the truth, even if he did not believe it. And so they did and, of course, he did not believe them!

As they left, Jerry said, 'Don't open the door. We'll meet you back here by ten.'

The next morning, the girls decided to listen at the stone door and then—if all was quiet—to go in and collect the hats and umbrellas and pillows. They had just reached the Temple when they found the bailiff, flat on his back. His forehead was cut and he bled a little.

The bailiff had obviously opened the door too early and been attacked by the Ugly-Wuglies. Jerry wet his handkerchief and the girls used that to wipe the bailiff's wound.

Cathy then sent Mabel to fetch from her aunt's house. The other three bent over the still-unconscious bailiff. Soon, a shadow fell on them and a voice spoke—but it was not Mabel's.

'Very sad affair,' it said. They looked up, into the face of the polite Ugly-Wugly. Jimmy and Cathy were terrified, but Jerry noticed that it just sounded like a normal person with a cold. The face was no longer a paper mask, but a real face, and the hands were real as well.

'How did it happen?' Jerry asked.

'The others must have lost their way last night. They never found the hotel,' said the Ugly-Wugly.

'Very respectable, by the way. Anyway, this morning, I found the others all at this door, very angry. Then this gentleman opened the door, and the tall man hit him on the head before I could protect him.'

By then, Jimmy was crying, so Jerry shoved the ring onto his brother's finger.

'I think the others have gone swimming. I saw their clothes in the wood,' continued the Ugly-Wugly.

While Jerry continued to dab the bailiff's head, the now-fearless Jimmy and Cathy

discovered the stuff that had been used to make the male Ugly-Wuglies.

'The spell's broken,' Cathy said, as they went back.

The bailiff regained consciousness just as Mabel returned. Jerry had prudently advised the Ugly-Wugly to hide in the bushes with Jimmy, when he saw the bailiff move. His excuse was that the man might not like strangers!

When he came to, the bailiff—like Eliza and Elf—thought it had been a dream.

Then, the children asked which way he was going and went the other way.

Later, just as Jerry suggested they seal up the ring in an envelope, Mabel had a thought.

'The ring is whatever you say it is!' she said. 'I said it was an invisible ring, so I became invisible.'

Everyone was hungry, so Mabel and Jerry went to the cottage and came back with food. As they ate, the girls told the boys how they had 'fed' the dinosaur. The children decided to collect the clothes and things from the dinosaur. Cathy took the ring from Mabel and raced to the dinosaur. When the boys caught up with her, Cathy said she would get the things because she knew where she had put everything. So Jerry gave her a boost, and soon it was raining clothes, hangers and hockey sticks.

Cathy was enjoying how cool it was inside the statue, and said, 'I suppose statues are always cool. I wish I was a statue. Oh!'

The 'Oh!' was cut off very short by a terrible silence. Cathy had got her wish.

'Jimmy,' Jerry said calmly, 'Cathy's gone and made herself a marble statue.'

Then, they broke the news to Mabel.

'How awful!' she said, and volunteered to stay with her.

'Good idea! But we'll come and check on you later,' said Jerry.

They decided to tell Mademoiselle that Cathy was spending the night in Yalding, which she certainly was!

Inside the dinosaur, Cathy was alive. It was warm and comfortable, and she soon fell asleep. Mabel slept among the bushes.

When Cathy awoke, she remembered she had been a statue inside the stone dinosaur.

She was just about to jump out when she realized the dinosaur had come alive! She dared not drop through the hole while the dinosaur was moving. It could crush her with its gigantic feet.

When she heard a splash, she dropped swiftly out of the hole and rolled to the side. She was just in time—she hadn't even stood up when the dinosaur slipped into the water and swam away.

The next moment, the laughing statue of Apollo jumped from his pedestal and landed nearby. He said hello and dived into the water, just like the dinosaur.

Cathy woke Mabel and said, 'Let's go home.'

'But Cathy!' Mabel said, 'You're still a statue. You've only come alive in the moonlight.'

Suddenly, a golden voice called out, 'Hello, little sister!'

It was Apollo! When Cathy introduced Mabel, Apollo asked how she could see him, without being afraid. Mabel showed him the ring.

Ah!' he said, 'but why haven't you become a statue also? Then we could all swim in the lake!'

'But we can't swim,' the girls said.

'You can,' said Apollo. 'All statues that come to life are expert athletes. And you, Mabel, need to wish exactly. Say "I wish that I may be a statue of living marble, but only till dawn".'

As soon as Mabel spoke the words, she became a live statue like Cathy. Apollo and the girls then jumped into the water, where the girls found they really could swim. Apollo told them to head to the central island, where they landed amid a fringe of fragrant plants. They went through a circular belt of trees, and the girls saw a round pool.

Beyond that, was a large group of twenty or thirty white statues—all alive. When they approached, Mabel placed a rose garland on each one's head. And the girls remembered Mademoiselle telling them how gods and goddesses always wore garlands. Then, Cathy wished the boys could be living statues like Mabel and her.

'Well, you could have simply wished them here,' Apollo said and asked—the statue with wings in the feet—to fly across and get them.

'And explain everything on the way,' he instructed.

By the time the marble Jerry and Jimmy arrived, each hanging onto one of Hermes's winged feet, they were perfectly at ease.

After the boys had eaten, the statue Queen Hera asked how the children had got the ring. Mabel told the story while the marble Olympians listened intently. Then, Mabel asked how they came alive, and what they knew about the ring. So Apollo began:

'All statues,' he said, 'can come alive at night, but the statues in ugly cities choose not to. You have seen us because you had the ring, and statues are like us, but on one night of the year, everyone can see us.'

'When is that?' Jerry asked politely.

'At the festival of the harvest,' said Apollo. 'On that night as the Moon rises it strikes one beam of perfect light on to the altar in certain temples. One of these temples is in this great garden. Not only that, on that night, we have to answer any question asked by a mortal.'

'When is that?'

But, just then, Zeus called for some music. Apollo said Zeus had to be obeyed, but told them to ask again before dawn. However, everyone was having such a good time, that dawn sneaked up on them before they realized it.

In an instant, all the statues had leaped to their feet and dived into the water. Only Hermes had a moment to hover above the children, since flying is faster than swimming.

'In fourteen days from now, at the Temple of Strange Stones,' he said before flying away.

Then the dawn came, and the children were back to normal.

'We should have gone with them. We can't even swim,' said Mabel.

They looked for a boat, but they could not find one. Disheartened, the four children started to explore the island. By now, the sun had risen. Jerry—who was leading the procession—was not looking where he was going. So he tripped and fell, and thus discovered a path.

'Oh yes,' said Mabel. 'There is a passage that goes under the water and comes out at the Temple of Flora. I'd forgotten all about it!'

The boys used the bicycle lamp they had brought to lead the girls through the underground passage.

Suddenly, the children found themselves in a great hall with an arched roof that was held up by two rows of round pillars. Every corner was filled with a soft, lovely light.

I will not describe it, because it looks different to different people. But there were many arches. And in each arch, was a picture showing the best that a soul of man could ask for, or that a man's destiny can grant: one had an olive garden, with two lovers holding hands in the moonlight. Another had a king on his throne. A third had the respectable Ugly-Wugly relaxing in a good hotel. And then, near the end of the hall, the children saw a statue of Psyche—the source of all this light! And she was still wearing the ring Cathy had given her to look at during the feast!

Jerry drew the ring off very gently, and Cathy took the ring and said, 'I wish we were safe in our own beds, in our nightgowns, and asleep.'

The next thing any of them knew, it was already morning and all of them were in their own beds. Cathy's only mistake had been in saying 'in our beds'. To this day Mabel's aunt cannot understand how Mabel, who had stayed over with those children, was in her bed in the morning.

***

The next morning, Mabel said she had told the bailiff about all their adventures.

'But I told him the absolute truth,' she said, 'so, naturally, he doesn't believe any of it.'

She had promised that they would all meet him for a picnic later, but since it was show-day, Mademoiselle was coming and wanted to walk back with the children. So Jerry volunteered to wait for her while the others went to meet the bailiff.

The picnic-tea was splendid, and Jimmy thought it was almost as good as the Immortals' feast. He told the bailiff so, but the latter did not believe him.

So he grabbed the ring from Cathy, showed it to the bailiff and told him to make a wish.

The bailiff put on the ring and said, 'I wish… I wish my friend was here.'

The children expected some confused man to show up but all they saw was Mademoiselle and Jerry, coming through the trees.

Jerry tried to introduce Mademoiselle to the bailiff, but the two of them just stood staring at each other.

Then, Mademoiselle said, 'I haven't seen Lord Yalding in a very long time!' and the two adults went for a walk.

'So that's Lord Yalding!' Jimmy said, stupefied.

'She's not his friend, she's his lover!' Mabel cried. 'She's the lady they put in the convent! And now they'll live happily ever after.'

One day, Jimmy overheard Lord Yalding say they could not get married because he was too poor. So the children showed him the secret treasures in the panelled room and gave him the magic ring.

That night, Lord Yalding put on the ring, saw the statues come alive and even shared in the Olympians' feast. When he told Mademoiselle all about it, she thought he was going mad! She was very worried.

On the night of the harvest festival, Mademoiselle and the four children met Lord Yalding at the Temple of Strange Stones—a ring of vast rugged stones, with a great flat stone in the middle.

When the moon rose, a single moonbeam hit the exact centre of flat stone only for a moment. And in that moment, everyone knew that they were somewhere where everything was easy and beautiful, even though no one could describe it properly.

After a while, Mademoiselle said softly, 'I want to go to the cave on the island.' So they did.

The hall of Psyche was as the children remembered—the Hall of Granted Wishes.

Then, a voice—that came from Mademoiselle, but it did not sound like her—said, 'The magic ring was given to your ancestor by a lady of my house so he could build her a garden and a house like the one in her own land. So this place was built partly by his love and partly by that magic. She never lived to see it; that was the price of the magic. Except from children, the ring exacts a payment from everyone else. I came here by your wish, and you paid with the madness that followed. Only one wish is free. Shall I wish it?'

'Yes!' they said.

'I wish, then,' said Lord Yalding's lover, 'that all the magic this ring has done may be undone, and that the ring itself may become a simple charm to bind you and me together for ever.'

As she stopped speaking, Psyche's light went out and the hall disappeared. Now, all that was left were a crude cave and Psyche's grave.

The next morning, many parts of the castle had disappeared as Lord Yalding's ancestor had used quite a bit of magic to build the place. The jewels were no longer in the panelled room, and there were not as many as before. But even those were enough to maintain the house and for Lord Yalding to marry his lover, which he did in a simple ceremony shortly thereafter.

The Hound of the Baskervilles

Arthur Conan Doyle

Sherlock Holmes was sitting at the breakfast table one morning when I picked up the walking stick that a visitor had accidentally left behind the previous night. The thick, round-headed stick had a broad silver band below its head. On it was written, 'To James Mortimer, MRCS, from friends at the CCH, and it was dated "1884".'

'Watson, what do you think of it?'

I wondered how Holmes—who had his back to me—knew what I was doing.

He quickly reassured me, 'I have a well-polished, silver coffee-pot before me. Now let's hear you reconstruct the person by examining his walking stick.'

'I think Dr Mortimer is an elderly, successful doctor, highly regarded because those who gave him this stick greatly appreciated him.'

'Excellent!' said Holmes.

I said, 'I also think that he is a country doctor who walks a lot.'

'Why?'

'Because the stick has been knocked around. This would not have happened if it belonged to a town doctor. Also, the iron cap is worn out.'

'Sound reasoning!' said Holmes.

'The "CCH", I fancy, must be the short form for Something Hunt, which we do not know yet,' I guessed.

'Watson, you're excelling yourself,' said Holmes.

Holmes took the stick and examined it for a while. Then he checked it again with a lens.

'Interesting, but elementary,' commented he. 'There are some signs on the stick which make me reach several deductions.'

'Have I missed out anything?' I asked with a degree of self-importance.

'Dear Watson, most of your deductions were wrong! But your errors sometimes lead me to the truth. Of course you are right in saying that Dr Mortimer is a country doctor who walks a lot.'

He said, 'But my dear Watson, that was not all. I would say that the presentation came from a hospital and not a hunt, and the initials "CCH" stand for the Charing Cross Hospital!'

'There's more,' Holmes carried on.

'When would a presentation like this be made? Apparently, when the good doctor left the hospital to start a practice in the countryside, he could not have been on the staff because only a well-established doctor in London could hold such a position. He may have been a house physician or a house-surgeon. Besides, he quit five years back—check the date on the walking stick. So your serious middle-aged doctor disappears into thin air and there appears a young man below thirty, unambitious, absent-minded, friendly, and one who has a favourite dog.'

I burst out laughing.

'It's easy to find out some details about our doctor's age and career,' Holmes said, as he blew smoke rings.

I fetched the medical directory and looked up several Mortimers and picked up the most likely one.

'James Mortimer, MRCS, 1882, Grimpen, Dartmoor, Devon,' I read aloud his record that also stated that he was a house surgeon at the Charing Cross Hospital, 1882–1884. He had also won an award and authored several medical essays.

Holmes smiled mischievously.

'What about the dog?' I asked.

'It could have been, and indeed it is a spaniel with curly hair!' replied Holmes. 'I know that because we have visitors, the doctor and his dog themselves!'

The doctor was very tall and thin, with a long beak-shaped nose, keen, grey eyes that were close-set and sparkled behind gold-rimmed spectacles.

When he saw his stick in Holmes's hand, he exclaimed happily, 'I'm so glad you have it! I wasn't sure where I left it.'

'Oh! My dear, that's not good!' Holmes said, when Dr Mortimer said that he was married. 'You have disturbed our deductions.'

'I left the hospital because of my marriage. I hoped to start a consultancy.'

The doctor went on to explain that he wanted to add Sherlock Holmes's skull to his anthropological museum after the detective died.

There was a moment of silence. Then, Holmes said, 'I presume that you didn't call only to examine my skull?'

'No, no,' Dr Mortimer said. 'I came because I am faced by a very extraordinary and serious problem.

'This family document was put in my care by Sir Charles Baskerville, whose tragic death three months back created lot of excitement in Devonshire. It's a statement of a legend which pertains to the Baskerville family,' Dr Mortimer said.

Holmes sat back, put the tips of his fingers together, and shut his eyes as Dr Mortimer read out the manuscript. It was written in old-fashioned script by one Hugo Baskerville to his sons, John and Rodger, with instructions that they must not tell their sister, Elizabeth, anything about it.

It said:

This story was told to me by my father who in turn got it from his father. It tells the terrible tale of our wicked ancestor, Hugo Baskerville—who shared my name—and explains the origin of the hound of the Baskervilles—a curse that has haunted us all these centuries.

Hugo, who owned the Baskerville Manor, was notorious for his wild and godless ways. Once, a beautiful, young village girl caught Hugo's eye but she refused his advances. So, he kidnapped her with help from his evil group of friends and they locked her up in a bedroom. Then, they proceeded to get quite drunk. The poor girl was terrified.

Luckily for her, there was a thick growth of ivy near her window. She used it to escape from them—but only for a while. When Hugo found that she had run away, he set the hounds after her.

Then the men mounted their horses and chased her down. They found her lying in a ditch, dead from fatigue and fear. They also found Hugo, who had been in the lead. His throat had been ripped out, and a huge, monstrous hound stood above him! Since then, several of our ancestors have died horrible deaths on the moor.

At the end of the story, Sherlock Holmes yawned and said that the manuscript would be interesting to a person who collected fairy tales.

Dr Mortimer did not say anything but produced a newspaper from his pocket.

'Holmes, this is more recent, from the *Devon County Chronicle* of May 14 this year. It is a brief report of the facts relating to the death of Sir Charles Baskerville,' he said.

Holmes looked at it and became more interested. He read the news item which stated:

> Sir Charles Baskerville's death has saddened the entire countryside. Though he lived for only two years at Baskerville Hall, Sir Charles helped everyone with his generosity and good nature.

A childless widower, he lived with Mr and Mrs Barrymore, who he employed as his butler and housekeeper, respectively. Sir Charles had a habit of taking an after-dinner walk down the Yew Alley and it was there that he was found dead—apparently of a cardiac arrest. Dr James Mortimer has testified to this effect and stated that Sir Charles had showed signs of this illness in the past. Sir Charles leaves behind his younger brother's son, Mr Henry Baskerville, who is believed to be living in America.

Sherlock Holmes thanked the good doctor and said, 'The case does present certain features of interest. Now tell me the private facts of the case.'

'The moor is thinly inhabited except for Mr Frankland, of Lafter Hall and the naturalist, Mr Stapleton, no educated men live there,' Dr Mortimer said.

'Recently, Sir Charles's nerves were on edge. He believed in the legend and was certain that a terrible curse hung over his family.'

'When I examined the spot where Sir Charles died, I noted that Barrymore made one wrong statement at the enquiry. He said there were no prints on the ground near the body. But I observed a little distance away, fresh and sharp footprints.'

'A woman's or a man's?' Holmes asked.

Dr Mortimer looked at us oddly.

'They were the footprints of a gigantic hound!' he whispered.

I shook when I heard these words. The doctor's voice betrayed a thrill and Holmes was excited!

'How comes no one else saw the prints?'

'They were about twenty yards away from the body and apparently no one bothered to look there.'

The doctor went on, 'I discovered that before the dreadful event occurred, several persons had seen an animal like the Baskerville demon on the moor. They all agreed that the creature was huge, ghostly and gruesome!'

'Dr Mortimer if you feel that this creature is a supernatural being, why have you come to consult me?'

'I want you to advise me what to do when Sir Henry Baskerville, the heir, arrives today at Waterloo Station! He has apparently been in Canada and is an excellent fellow by all accounts.'

'He is the only heir to the Baskerville fortune?'

'Yes.'

'Then, sir,' said Holmes, 'I suggest that you meet Sir Henry Baskerville, and wait for twenty-four hours for my message about what to do next. Come over tomorrow, and please bring Sir Henry with you.'

I knew Holmes needed solitude to concentrate on the case, so I went out and returned to Baker Street late in the evening.

As I entered the house, Holmes unrolled a section of a big map of the district which concerned the case.

He said, 'That's Baskerville Hall in the centre, surrounded by a wood.'

'This small group of buildings here is the village of Grimpen, where Dr Mortimer has his practice. This is Lafter Hall and a house which could belong to Stapleton, the naturalist. Fourteen miles further is the huge prison of Princetown. This is the stage on which our tragedy was played.'

Our clients arrived punctually the next morning. The baronet was small, alert and dark-eyed, about thirty years old, very tough with thick black eyebrows and had a tough face.

Sir Henry immediately got down to business.

'A strange thing has happened,' he said. 'No one knows where I am staying, but I received a note at my hotel which read:

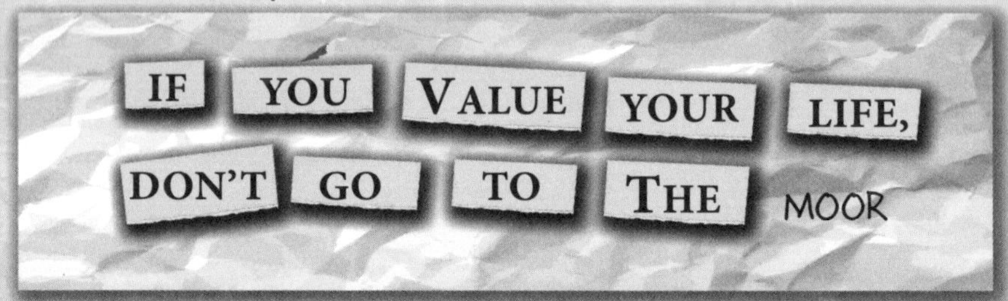

The last word was written in ink, the other words were cut and pasted.

Holmes commented, 'Somebody is apparently very interested in your movements.'

Holmes then asked me to read the lead editorial in the *Times*. None of us could make any sense of it, but Holmes soon pointed out the words, 'value', 'your', 'life', etc., which appeared in the note that Sir Henry received.

'The author had to write down "moor" for that's a word that's tough to find in a newspaper,' he concluded.

'Has anything else extraordinary happened after you reached London?' Holmes asked the baronet.

'I lost one of my boots!' he said, but Dr Mortimer scolded him for troubling Holmes with such unnecessary details.

Holmes then proceeded to tell Sir Henry the entire story of the Baskerville curse, since the latter did not know anything about it.

Sir Henry listened with great attention and showed his surprise from time to time.

'Sir Henry, it is advisable for you not to travel alone to Baskerville Hall,' Holmes said.

This angered the fiery baronet.

'There is no evil spirit in hell, or man on earth who can stop me from going to my own people's home!' he exclaimed. He later invited Holmes and me to lunch.

As soon as Dr Mortimer and Sir Henry left, Holmes leapt into action. His aim was to track the author of the letter who, he was sure, would be following Sir Henry. We saw a man with a black beard in a cab, but he noticed us and instructed the driver to flee.

However, Holmes had taken down the cab's number—2704. We then went to a messenger office, where Holmes instructed Cartwright, the manager's son, to check the garbage bins of all the hotels in Charing Cross and look for a torn copy of the *Times*. He also said that we would check on the cab number before going for lunch.

When Cartwright informed Holmes that there were twenty-three hotels in Charing Cross, the detective handed him twenty-three shillings—one for each of the hotel porters to check the garbage bins for the centre page of the newspaper.

Holmes added, 'Report to me at Baker Street by wire before evening.'

We then went to keep our lunch appointment with Sir Henry at the Northumberland Hotel.

As we climbed up the stairs, we ran into Sir Henry himself. He was very angry, was holding an old boot in his hand!

'This is too much!' said he. 'First my new boot is stolen and now my old one!'

'A strange thing,' said Holmes, thoughtfully. 'I cannot understand it. Your case is complex indeed, Sir Henry!'

Sir Henry said he was going to Baskerville Hall at the end of the week.

Holmes said, 'You have been chased by strange people in London but in this great city of millions it is hard to learn who they are or what their object is.'

To Dr Mortimer, Mr Holmes said, 'You were followed from my house this morning.'

Dr Mortimer recoiled violently.

'By whom?'

'Do you have any neighbours at Dartmoor with full, black full beards?'

'Yes, there's Barrymore, Sir Charles's butler.'

'Where is he now?'

'Looking after Baskerville Hall.'

'I'll send a telegram to confirm this,' Holmes said.

On questioning Mortimer about Sir Charles's will, Holmes learnt that Barrymore and his wife would gain £500 each; Dr Mortimer himself £1,000; big sums went to charities and £740,000 to Sir Henry.

'And if Sir Henry would die, who would profit?'

'Sir Charles's younger brother Rodger Baskerville died unmarried and so the estate would go to the Desmonds, their distant cousins. James Desmond is an old clergyman in Westmoreland. James Desmond is a respected man who refused to accept a settlement from Sir Charles.'

Sir Henry said, 'I have not made my will yet, but I feel that the inheritance must go with the estate and title so that the glories of the Baskervilles are restored. Dr Mortimer is returning with me to Devon.'

'Since Dr Mortimer has a busy practice and lives several miles from your house, I would suggest you also take someone else—like Dr Watson!' said Holmes.

'It will be my pleasure,' said I, in anticipation of good adventure.

Suddenly Sir Baskerville cried out in triumph! He found his new boot under a cabinet!

The mystery of the boot could not be solved and before dinner the arrival of two telegrams caught our attention. The first stated that Barrymore was at the Hall.

The second said that the sender had gone to twenty-three hotels but was unable to find any cut-out *Times* newspaper.

'Two of my leads are gone,' lamented Holmes.

Soon, the third also vanished when the cab owner, John Clayton, rushed in to say that the bearded man who hired his vehicle said that he was a detective and that his name was Sherlock Holmes!

Holmes was stunned when he heard this, but burst out laughing at the boldness of the bearded stranger!

'I want you to only report the facts of the case in full. Let me do the theorizing,' was Holmes's advice to me as I prepared to leave for Baskerville Hall with the baronet.

'Carry your revolver all the time and don't let your guard down,' added he.

The train journey was pleasant and swift, and a carriage was waiting for us at the railway station. We were enjoying the drive when suddenly Dr Mortimer cried out, 'What's this?'

Along the road, a few policemen were watching us and Dr Mortimer was surprised.

The driver answered, 'A convict, Selden—the Notting Hill killer—has escaped from Princetown, and has been on the run for three days. They're searching for him.'

Finally we were there—Baskerville Hall.

The lodge was in bad shape but opposite it was a half-constructed new building.

'Welcome to Baskerville Hall, Sir Henry!' said the tall butler Barrymore as he stepped out to open the wagon door. His wife the housekeeper helped him carry our bags.

Dr Mortimer went straight home as his wife was waiting for him.

Barrymore was a striking man with distinguished features and, of course, a full black beard. He took no time in making clear what his wife and he intended to do soon.

'You will need to hire new servants,' he said, 'for my wife and I wish to leave and start a small business for ourselves. Of course, only when it's convenient to you, sir. We were very attached to Sir Charles and his tragic end has made this place very painful for us to live in anymore.'

Late that night I was disturbed by the sobbing of a woman. It was the choking sound of a person torn by a great sorrow. The noise came from somewhere in the house.

***

The following morning, both Sir Henry and I conceded that we had heard a woman weeping the night before. Mrs Barrymore's swollen red eyes indicated she was the one who was crying.

Sir Henry had some paperwork to attend to, so I decided to go on a walk in the pleasant countryside. Soon, I reached the Grimpen post office where the postmaster's boy told me that Barrymore had been at home when he delivered Mr Holmes's telegram.

'Did you give it to him in his hand?'

'No,' the boy said, 'but his wife said he was in the loft and she would deliver it to him.'

I was confused and wished Mr Holmes were at my side then.

At that moment, a stranger called out my name and came up to me. He had a butterfly net in his hand, and introduced himself as Stapleton. Dr Mortimer had mentioned about him and told us that he was a naturalist. Stapleton then asked me about Sir Henry and said he hoped the young baronet would continue the good work that Sir Charles had started.

Then he said, 'I think all this talk about something fearful bringing about Sir Charles's death was rubbish.'

I was surprised that Stapleton knew about Sir Charles's medical condition, but the naturalist said, 'Dr Mortimer had told me about it.'

Stapleton spoke about the danger and mystery of the moor and pointed to me the Great Grimpen Mire—a stretch of quicksand. Suddenly a low, moaning sound was heard, and Stapleton said, 'The locals believe this is the sound of the Hound of the Baskervilles!'

The naturalist suddenly went chasing a butterfly and we were soon in the company of his sister, Miss Beryl Stapleton, a dark-eyed beauty.

As I tried to introduce myself, she cut me short and strangely said, 'Go back to London immediately! Return at once. The moor is not the place for you! Please don't tell my brother that I have said this to you.'

Soon, Stapleton joined us again and I learnt that his sister had mistaken me for Sir Henry!

Later when I was returning to the Hall, Miss Stapleton sought me out and told me, 'Please forget what I told you.'

I was more surprised than ever!

From now onwards, I will continue this strange and gripping tale in the manner in which I reported the course of events to Holmes, that is, in the form of letters.

October 13
My Dear Holmes,

The moor is indeed a lonely place. One can imagine prehistoric men suddenly coming out and confronting you. It sometimes is unnerving!

The locals believe that the escaped convict left the area a fortnight back, which has greatly relieved them. He could, of course, be hiding in one of the many stone huts here, but the lack of food would force him away.

The baronet has started to show great interest in Miss Stapleton, which is not surprising considering the loneliness of this place—and the attractiveness of the lady! She has a hidden fire within herself! Her brother has a huge influence over her. It is seen in his eyes, as if he is giving approval to whatever she has to say.

I met another neighbour—Frankland of Lafter Hall. He lives four miles away south. He is elderly, white-haired, red-faced and moody. His passion is litigation and he has spent plenty of money in it. He appears to be a good-natured soul and I mention him for you wanted every bit of information that I could gather.

***

October 15
My Dear Holmes,

The other night, I saw Barrymore moving slowly in the house. The next morning, I examined the window through which he had been staring out. It gives the nearest view of the moor. Undoubtedly, Barrymore must have been looking for somebody or something there! I felt there was some love triangle involved. I spoke to Sir Henry about it and he said he would talk to Barrymore about it for he too had seen his butler move around similarly about the house at night.

That night, we both followed Barrymore as he took his walk. When he reached that particular window he waved his candle as if signalling somebody. When he saw us, Barrymore started shaking. Sir Henry asked him, 'Barrymore, what are you doing?'

'Sir, I check the windows to see if they are latched', he replied.

'But this is the second floor!'

'Barrymore,' the baronet said strictly, 'I want the truth!'

Persistent questioning brought forth nothing and it was Mrs Barrymore who came out of her room to unravel the mystery.

She admitted, 'It's my younger brother, sir; he's the convict Selden they are looking for. He was pampered when he was young and fell in with thieves and murderers. I have taken care of him when he was a child and I cannot see him perish without any food out there on the moor.'

'Watson, get your revolver. We must seek the convict out. He is a threat to us and the Stapletons!' Sir Henry told me.

We searched the dark and dreadful surrounding and finally found him! Selden's face was evil; his beard had grown and his hair was matted. He looked like a savage but proved to be strong and agile, for he darted away from us after flinging a stone which broke up on the rock that sheltered us. Though we chased him hard, we soon lost him in the misty moor.

It was someone else who caught our attention! In the distance we saw a tall figure emerge, and quickly go out of sight!

The next morning Barrymore said he had some information.

'It's about the death of poor Sir Charles,' he said.

Sir Henry rose up instantly, 'What is it?'

'I know that he was at the gate at that time. He was waiting to meet a woman.'

'Her name?'

'I can only give you her initials—LL. I know this for he got a letter from Coombe Tracey written in a woman's hand.'

I met Dr Mortimer later that day and he revealed this information. He told me, 'Her name is Laura Lyons. She is the daughter of Mr Frankland. She married an artist against her father's wishes and he disowned her. Later, her husband also abandoned her and she met Sir Charles, who promised to help her financially.'

I left at once for Coombe Tracey and met the beautiful brunette, Laura Lyons. She was initially suspicious but later became cooperative and admitted that Sir Charles helped her with money and that she wrote to him a couple of times.

When I pressed the matter, she said that Stapleton had told Sir Charles about her situation.

'I wrote that letter to Sir Charles, but did not keep the appointment. I had heard that the baronet was leaving for London the next morning and that's why I decided not to meet him so late and at such an odd place,' she said.

'The letter was an appeal for money, which I managed to get from another source.'

Frustrated, I decided to seek out the mysterious tall man on the moor. I headed for the hut where I presumed he was put up, but no one was there. Suddenly I heard a shout of greeting behind me! It was Holmes!

The detective showed great pleasure on meeting me and had given instructions in London to redirect

my communications to him so that my work did not go in vain. He said he had stayed in a hut on the moor so that his enemies would not know that he was involved in this great mystery. I also learned from Holmes that Beryl Stapleton, who mistook me for Sir Henry, was actually Stapleton's wife!

Holmes said, 'I investigated Mr Stapleton's background. He used to be a schoolmaster in the north. He is so wicked that he has used his wife and Laura to lure Sir Charles to his doom!'

Holmes decided we must visit Laura Lyons again, to expose Stapleton and to hopefully, change her loyalties.

Our thoughts were preoccupied with these matters when suddenly a man's loud scream

was heard on the moor. We ran to investigate and discovered the convict, dead! He had been wearing Sir Henry's old clothes!

It turned out that Barrymore had passed on the Baronet's old clothes to his fugitive brother-in-law Selden and the hound—having sniffed Henry's boot that was stolen in London—had attacked the wrong man because he was wearing the right clothes!

Stapleton showed up at this precise moment and assumed that it was Sir Henry who had been killed. He sputtered 'Who-Who' when we told him that it was the escaped convict.

I asked the naturalist, 'Why did you think it was Sir Henry?'

'I had asked him to come to my place, that's why,' Stapleton answered.

Holmes then guided the conversation away from that topic.

'Selden probably fell and broke his neck,' he explained, adding, 'Mr Stapleton, I intend to return to London tomorrow. The situation here is too full of myths and I'm not interested in the fairy-tales that plague this case.'

'I marvel at the man's self-control,' Holmes remarked, as we walked back.

I said, 'I wonder whether Stapleton will be more cautious or become more desperate now that he has seen you. I think you should arrest him, Holmes.'

'How?' Holmes asked. 'We don't have any proof of his guilt.'

Holmes put hope in the meeting with Mrs Lyons, but revealed that he had another plan too.

'Watson, don't tell Henry of Selden's death. And excuse me from the dinner which Henry and I were to attend at Stapleton's tomorrow.'

Holmes quietly broke the news of her brother's death to Mrs Barrymore and looked keenly at a portrait on the wall of Sir Hugo Baskerville.

Holmes told me, 'Look at how similar Hugo Baskerville and Stapleton look! It is obvious that they are related; it also explains Stapleton's motive in this horrible affair—it is obvious he wanted the inheritance.'

When Holmes told Mrs Lyons that Stapleton was married to Beryl, she was so shocked she did not believe it. Once Holmes produced a photo of the Stapleton—husband and wife—however, Laura spilled the beans.

Stapleton had promised to marry her if she got a divorce, for which she needed Sir Charles's help. The naturalist made Laura write the letter to Sir Charles, and then forced her to miss the appointment. He also threatened Laura, saying she would get into trouble if she did not keep quiet.

Later, Holmes's plan was put into action. Three of us—Holmes, Detective Lestrade of the London Police and I—tiptoed our way to Merripit House, where Stapleton and his wife stayed. We hid behind some rocks and observed Stapleton and Sir Henry chatting over coffee. Sir Henry seemed nervous, probably thinking about the long walk home across the moor.

Stapleton suddenly got up and headed to a small shed, from where we heard some strange noises. By now, a thick fog was settling across the moor, and we were getting worried as the visibility became worse. If the fog were to engulf the path from Merripit House to Baskerville Hall, no one would be able to watch Sir Henry's walk home or protect him when the hound attacked.

As it was, the fog had completely covered the path when Sir Henry started his walk and we heard the sound of the hound before we saw it!

When it did emerge from the mist, the creature took our breath away! It was a huge, glowing, fire-breathing beast—just what the Baskerville myth predicted.

Stunned, we could only shoot one round of bullets as the hound nipped at Sir Henry's heels. The shots did not kill the beast, and it leapt at the baronet's throat. But Holmes managed to fire five more rounds at the right moment and the hound collapsed!

The baronet suffered no injuries. The animal was a mix of a mastiff and a bloodhound. It was as big as a lion and covered with phosphorous to make it glow. In the house, we discovered Mrs Stapleton gagged and bound.

Her husband had tied her up because she wanted to help Sir Henry, she revealed. She also told us about her husband's hiding place in the Grimpen Mire, where he kept his hound. Deciding that the fog was too thick to pursue the villain, Holmes and I headed back to Baskerville Hall with Sir Henry.

The next day Mrs Stapleton led us through a safer path across the quicksand. Stapleton himself could not be discovered and we presumed that the Great Grimpen Mire had swallowed him. We also found the phosphorous used to make the beast shine—which made it scary enough to frighten Sir Charles to death.

***

Back in London, Holmes explained that Stapleton was actually the son of Roger Baskerville, Charles's younger brother who moved to South America and was presumed dead. Stapleton, or Sir Roger Baskerville, Jr, lived in South America and married Beryl Garçia of Costa Rica, the dark beauty who was disguised as his sister. Roger fled to England after stealing public money, changed his name and established a school. When the school opened, Roger headed to Devonshire where he had heard of his stake in a large inheritance. Having befriended Sir Charles, Roger heard of the myth of the hound and of Charles's bad heart.

To get the superstitious Charles out alone on the moor, Stapleton tried to enlist his wife, but she refused. He happened, however, to meet Laura Lyons, and he told her he would marry her if she got a divorce. Convincing her to get the necessary money from Charles, he made her miss the late-night appointment and let loose his hound.

Once Sir Henry arrived on the scene, Stapleton took his wife with him to London, where he followed the baronet. Stapleton also made a point of stealing one of Sir Henry's shoes to give his hound the baronet's scent. However, the first boot he stole was brand new, not yet worn by Sir Henry and unsuitable for its intended purpose. The note that Sir Henry had received had come from Mrs Stapleton trying to prove Stapleton's guilt, and Holmes had used Sir Henry as a bait to catch Stapleton red-handed.

Other Titles *in the* Series

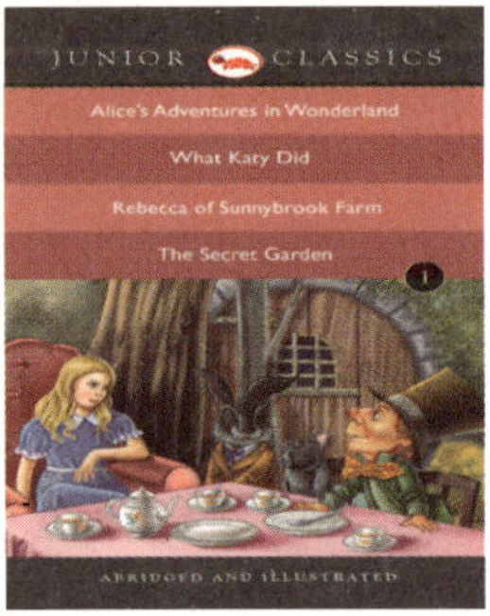

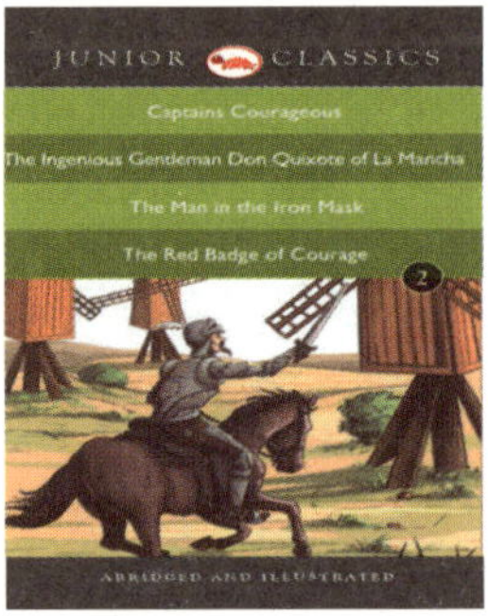

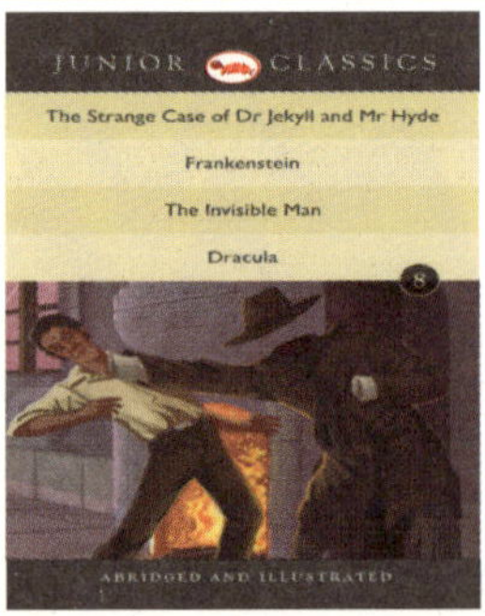